True Dark

"Admirers of Mike Miner's previous novels will undergo quick conversions to devoted fans when they read *True Dark*. Everything Miner does well—the spare dialogue loaded to within an inch of mercy, a story that doesn't so much unfold as uncoil, breathtaking tension—he has sharpened to a masterful art in *True Dark*. That Miner does this without ever letting go of your heart, no matter how jaded, is the mark of emerging genius."

—James Anderson, author of
The Never-Open Desert Diner

"A carefully calibrated and complex page-turner that cascades over generations and decades without ever losing intensity. Miner keeps upping his game. Plot lines, eras, and characters interlace effortlessly in a well-crafted page-turner. Miner's skills have out-paced his peers. *True Dark* is a perfect crime novel."

—Tom Pitts, author of *101*

TRUE DARK

MIKE MINER

TRUE DARK

All Due Respect
An imprint of Down & Out Books
3959 Van Dyke Rd, Ste. 265
Lutz, FL 33558
www.DownAndOutBooks.com

Cover image credit Gareth McGorman
Cover design by JT Lindroos

ISBN: 1-64396-045-8
ISBN-13: 978-1-64396-045-6

1

1980

Leo Murphy was eight years old the first time his brother, Ryan, saved his life. Ryan was thirteen.

They lived with their father in Oscuro, California on the very western edge of the Sonora Desert, in the shadow of the Oscuro Mountain range, spitting distance from the Mexican border. The town was home to a few hundred hardy souls who preferred land and sky to people. Folks who felt crowded when in groups bigger than two handfuls.

The nearest Dairy Queen was over an hour's drive northeast in Quicksilver, right next to the nearest hospital. It was a drive the boys made only on their birthdays. The trip was made longer by Leo's carsickness. Halfway there they would have to stop and give him some fresh air. They learned the hard way on his fifth birthday when their father chose not to stop and Leo vomited all over the dashboard of their father's blue Ford pickup. The smell of it, even with both windows open, nearly

1

spoiled their appetites for ice cream. Nearly.

Their mother passed away when Leo was five. He had no real memories of her. Cancer, which their father swore was a result of the mercury mines, now long abandoned, that dotted Oscuro County. Including one on their own land which had once been the biggest supplier of cinnabar in the country. A lot of people had gotten sick digging it out of the ground. Their grandfather had made a lot of money before it closed.

"What was she like?" Leo would ask his father and brother from time to time.

"Beautiful," they usually said, which was proven in the pictures of her on his daddy's dresser and on the living room walls, or "Kind."

"She was crazy for stars," Ryan told him one night.

"Stars?"

"She loved to sit outside at night and stargaze. She'd point to different constellations, name them. Ursa Major, the big bear. Scorpius, the scorpion. She named me Orion after the hunter. You're Leo, the lion." Ryan pointed up to the constellation he was named after, made up of fifteen stars.

Orion had been too odd a name for the locals and had soon become Ryan for everyone but their mother—and sometimes their father.

Tonight there were no stars, no moon, invisible clouds crowded the sky. There is not a more perfect darkness in all the world than on a moonless, starless night in Oscuro, California. Ryan and Leo stared out into the ink. Their daddy was out on a call. He was the county sheriff, which wasn't saying much, but there was a propensity for violence in this region, as if the spilled blood of massacred Kumeyaay Indians and the blood of those massacred by Kumeyaay were the source of some mysterious virus that caused short tempers and itchy trigger fingers.

"Mighty dark out there," Ryan said.

Leo's belly tingled at the mischief in his brother's voice. "Like somebody painted the windows black."

"Feller'd have to be awful stupid to go out into that kind of a night."

"Or awful brave," Leo said.

"Oh, I don't know anybody that brave."

"You know me, don't you?"

"You're saying you'd go out in that?"

"I would and I'm gonna," Leo said. "And I dare you to do the same."

"You dare me?"

"I double dare you."

"No flashlight?"

"Nope. And barefoot."

Even Ryan paused at that condition. "Barefoot?"

"Whatsamatter, big brother? Scared?"

"Not even a little."

But they both were. They pictured the creatures that crept and crawled and slithered among the rocks and sand around their home. As Leo stepped toward the door he searched his mind for a way out of this challenge without losing face. He couldn't help himself. Always felt the need to look tough in front of Ryan. Neither of them would ever refuse a dare.

The linoleum floor in the kitchen was cool against the soles of their feet. Before stepping outside, Ryan turned off the porch light.

The boys were blind. The world was suddenly snatched away, held behind some sinister being's back.

Leo closed his eyes then opened them. No difference. He waited to see if shapes would emerge once his eyes adjusted but none did. Ryan touched his shoulder and Leo jerked.

"Easy, little brother." The familiar voice was a small comfort.

"We walk straight out. You get scared, you get hurt, you call my name. Got it?"

Leo nodded, a useless gesture.

"You got it?"

"I got it."

"Then get goin', tough guy."

One tentative step. Then another. The night was made of wind that swirled around him. From above, the windmill's blades whirred. Leo moved into the deepest dark he'd ever known, dizzy without a horizon for reference. Only the rough ground under his toes. A creak as the wind shifted making the weathervane on top of their barn change direction.

He pictured scorpions beneath every step. Did they come out at night? In the distance, a coyote howled. Maybe it was scared of the dark too. Would howling make him feel better? Where was Ryan? He wanted to call to him, just to see where he was, but realized he would lose the dare if he did.

A few more steps. A sharp rock made him groan. He needed to pee. Could he just go for it right here? Why not? He unzipped, felt the wind on his privates, aimed his piss in the other direction. That's better, he thought.

Then the unmistakable sound of a snake's rattle.

Terror spread from his ears down his spine out to his limbs, to his fingers and toes. The dark suddenly close, he felt trapped. The stream of his urine slowed, hot drips hit his feet.

Another rattle made the boy recoil but he'd lost his sense of direction, didn't know where the snake was, didn't know where home was, the sound seemed to be inside his head. He wanted to scream but sobs choked him. Where was Ryan? His eyes strained to see. He thought he heard the rattler slither toward him. When it rattled again, he finally gasped out his brother's name.

"Ryan?"

The air reminded him of all his exposed parts, he wanted to lie in a fetal position, turn into a turtle, but he was too scared to move.

Two fangs sank into the tight flesh above his ankle.

Sometimes the actual thing we fear is not as bad as we think it will be. A rattlesnake bite is much worse. Because it is not over after the bite. The venom has work to do.

Leo's screams stabbed the night.

The kitchen light came on, closer than Leo would ever have thought. Ryan's silhouette approached, fast. It was hard for Leo to notice anything besides his pain.

Ryan touched his brother's shoulder. "Did he get you?"

"It hurts, Ryan."

"Where is he?"

The snake's rattle answered him.

Ryan fired his father's shotgun at the creature.

"Can you walk?"

He tried. "It hurts."

"Okay." Ryan put his arm around Leo to support him.

The small light in their small house looked pitiful to Leo who winced as he limped with his brother's help. One dim light, hopeless, in the middle of an ocean of darkness. Their nearest neighbors, the Potters, lived a bunch of miles south.

"What are we going to do?"

"Wait here?"

"Where are you going?"

Leo thought of his mother. Would that be all that remained of him? Some pictures on the wall. The memories of his father and brother. Would he be buried next to his mother, in the family plot? What would his tombstone read? Beloved son and brother?

He heard the whine of the passenger door of his father's old pickup opening. The dome light popped on. They called the truck Blue Thunder. Ryan dropped the shotgun and pulled and pushed his little brother into the seat. Leo looked at the puckered wound above his ankle, already swelling, the skin wrinkling and buckling strangely, like it had been doused with acid. Ryan slammed the door and ran to the driver's side.

When Ryan turned the key and hit the gas, the engine rumbled, living up to its nickname. Reluctantly it turned over and roared to life.

"Where are we going?"

"The hospital. You're gonna be okay."

Ryan, tall for his age, could just reach the pedals. Their father taught him how to drive a few months ago so Ryan could help him maintain the fence that bordered their property. He'd never driven on the road before. He turned on the headlights and touched the gas. The steering wheel looked so big in his hands.

Ryan followed the beams into the vastness in front of them, the dirt road eventually turned into pavement, the only proof that they weren't on the moon or mars. Not another vehicle, not another light or structure in sight.

Halfway there the adrenaline wore off and Ryan

got sleepy. The truck drifted onto the rocky shoulder, startling him awake.

Leo's ankle swelled and the skin burned. He tried to watch where they were going but his vision blurred. He slipped in and out of consciousness. In his dreams his mother spoke to him, her voice familiar, almost forgotten, comforting. *I should have been there for you, my sweet little boy.*

"You are here, Mom."

Her face was black-and-white, like her pictures, but sad.

"Sing me a song."

Leo was startled when Ryan started to hum, *My home's in Montana. I wear a bandanna. My spurs are of silver. My pony is gray.*

"Do you hear her too?"

To the west, strange lights, like tiny moons, appeared out of the night.

"Holy crap," Ryan said.

"What is it?"

"I've heard of them but never seen 'em before."

"What?"

"They call them the San Diablo lights."

They floated, eerie and pale, vaporous, just above the horizon. Leo counted six.

"What's making them?"

"Nobody knows. UFOs, some people say. The Indians thought they were fallen stars. Pretty spooky."

As they drove, the lights moved, changed shape

and color. Was this a sign, Leo wondered, from the other side? Or a warning? He decided to take comfort in them, in their mystery. The lights followed him into his sleep, kept his darkest thoughts at bay.

Leo woke to the sound of cars honking, the truck jerking. In Quicksilver, Ryan struggled to follow the street signs and lights, to stay inside the lines, there was too much to process. Leo looked at the speedometer. They were going fifteen miles per hour.

His ankle was the size and shape of a football. His skin was the color of red coals and felt as hot.

Were those tears in Ryan's eyes?

The world changed color, flashed blue and red, then blue again. A siren whined. A police car, right behind them. Ryan pulled over. Wiped his face with his sleeve.

The cop was young, blonde hair cut military short. His shirt and pants were a bit too big. He tapped on the window. Ryan rolled it down.

"You boys out for a joyride?"

Ryan wept and pointed to his brother's leg.

The cop shined his flashlight on the wound. Sucked in a breath. "I'll be right back." He ran to his car, turned off the flashing lights and ran back to their truck. "Slide over, kid."

He gunned the engine. "Where you boys from?"

"Oscuro," Ryan said.

"You two drove up here from Oscuro?"

"I drove."

"How old are you?"

"Thirteen."

"Where's mom and dad?"

"Dad's at work. He's the sheriff."

The cop's eyes widened. "You're Jeremiah Murphy's kids?"

"Yes sir."

Up ahead Leo saw the Dairy Queen. The hospital was right next to it.

"What are your names?"

"I'm Ryan, this is Leo."

"I'm Glenn. Pleased to meet you. Leo, how you holdin' up?"

"Okay."

"You got a helluva brave brother. You know that?"

The heat in Leo's ankle moved to his chest. Pride. "Yes sir."

"Good. Not everyone's brother woulda saved your life tonight."

They pulled into a place that said *Ambulances Only*. The looks of confusion on the hospital staff's faces turned to focus and concern when they saw Leo's wound. A huge black man in white scrubs lifted the boy out of the truck, speaking in a gentle voice, "Okay, son." He placed Leo on a gurney. Ryan scooted out of the cab and stood next to his brother.

"Howdy, Glenn. What we got here?"

Glenn came around the truck. "Just what you see, Vernon. The snake bit one's Leo. That's his brother, Ryan."

Ryan looked up at Vernon. "Is my brother gonna be okay?"

Vernon put a big paw on Ryan's shoulder. "We've seen a lot worse than this, believe it or not. We'll get him fixed up. Now follow me." He pushed the gurney through the automatic doors of the hospital.

Ryan turned back to Glenn. "You coming?"

Glenn sighed. "I'm coming."

The hospital's sudden brightness hurt Leo's eyes, fluorescent light shouted against the too-white walls, and when he shut his eyes, he could still hear them buzz and hiss. Motion everywhere, rooms full of emergencies, the gurney wheels squealed like a maniac's laughter through the hallways.

It felt as though someone had taken an iron out of a fire and was holding it against his ankle. The pain and the lights made his eyes tear.

"It hurts."

"It looks like it hurts, kid."

Leo tried to lift his head to see.

Vernon gently pushed his chest down. "What you wanna do that for? Listen. You in the right place. Doc gonna fix you up. You'll be dancing outta here."

"I can't dance."

"Not yet."

Behind them, Ryan and Glenn followed, Glenn with his arm around the teenager.

Vernon brought them into a room with a bed and some chairs.

"Here we go." He lifted Leo onto the bed, adjusted it so his back was raised.

"Shouldn't we lift the leg?" Glenn said.

"Not for a snake bite, Deputy."

Glenn nodded.

"Okay then. Doc'll be here directly. Might see a nurse or two. They'll treat you right. They don't, you tell ol' Vernon about it." He lifted a device with buttons on it. "Something serious happens, you buzz the nurse, here." An orange button with a cartoon nurse.

Ryan said, "How do we know if it's serious?"

"You'll know. Don't worry, Leo. You'll feel better soon. We'll work on those dance moves." While they waited, Glenn made a phone call, twisting the rotary dial as fast as it would go. He spoke to a woman named Maggie about getting hold of their father. Doctor Helfrick arrived a minute later. He resembled a slender Santa Claus, with a well-trimmed snowy beard framing his smile. "Guns and snakes. Two things boys shouldn't play with." He looked at the chart. "Which one of y'all's Leo?"

Leo looked at him like he was crazy. "I am, Doctor."

"You sure?"

"Yes sir."

"Good." His eyes were so blue, they were almost colorless. He winked at the boy. "Well what the hell happened?"

"Got the wrong end of a rattler."

"Looks like it." He inspected the wound with a sour expression. "Yup. That's just what happened. How's your vision?" He pulled a pen light out of his coat pocket and clicked it on.

"Okay."

"Follow the light." He shined the light in his eyes moving it left and right, up and down, then clicked it off. "Good." He put his stethoscope on his ears then rubbed the metal head to warm it up and placed it against Leo's chest. "Gimme some deep breaths."

A nurse entered while Leo was inhaling.

Doctor Helfrick put a hand on the boy's head. "I think you're gonna live, Leo."

The phone rang. Glenn picked it up. "Glenn here." He listened. "Thanks, Maggie. You're a peach."

Everyone looked at Glenn with expectant eyes.

"Daddy's on the way, kids."

Leo looked at Ryan. Not exactly relief in their eyes. Their mother's death had taken a deep bite out of their daddy's heart, worse even than Leo's rattlesnake bite. The venom that now ran through his veins turned him ornery, made him impatient and mean. They saw it in his eyes. Where once they'd found love mixed with the sternness, now they saw anger. His eyes looked first for what was wrong, and always found something.

When Leo dropped a plate in the kitchen, shattering it, the slap to his temple had been swift and hard. "Don't just stand there and cry. Clean it up."

Ryan would always try to turn his father's temper on himself. "Wow, you really showed him, Daddy."

"Say that again."

"You getting hard of hearing, old man?"

Their father knocked a chair over leaping at his son. He struck Ryan's head with a fist. "Don't you dare disrespect me in my own house."

Ryan covered up but took what his father dished out. Finally, winded, his father stopped. Hunched over, hands on his knees, breathing heavy.

Leo picked up the big pieces of porcelain, then got a broom and dustpan and swept up the little shards. The only noises the stiff bristles against the linoleum floor, Ryan and their daddy's heavy breathing, the blood pounding in Leo's ears.

Daddy's expression then full of regret and something else. Fear. In his troubled dreams, Leo would see the three of them, father and two sons, in a small boat in a raging storm, waves that reached the clouds, then crashed onto them. In the brief lightning flashes that illuminated the darkness, he would see that expression on his daddy's face.

Try as Leo might to hate his daddy, he couldn't get the image of a man lost at sea out of his head. So he just felt sorry for him. And himself.

Ryan was much better at hating his daddy. He took his beatings without complaint or comment.

Leo felt sorry for him too.

Maybe Daddy didn't like what he saw in the mirror, the eyes that scared his boys, maybe they scared him as well. Daddy began to hit the bottle. Jim Beam on ice. It made him unpredictable, as likely to cry as shout. They were always aware of him, careful not to provoke him, like a wild animal loose in the house.

His occasional calls to emergencies, domestic disputes or fires or robberies, became welcome respites. Ryan would put Leo to bed, read him a story. On those nights Leo slept without dreams. And it allowed them to play without fearing their daddy's wrath.

Like tonight.

But now Daddy was on his way. They took deep breaths, and worried.

Even before they could hear him, they could sense a heaviness in the air.

He barged into the room, red-faced, eyes bloodshot. "What the fuck happened?"

Glenn stood, appraised the situation. He looked at the boys, neither of whom took their eyes off their father.

"I'm sorry, Daddy."

"Sheriff Murphy, I'm Glenn Daniels." He held out his hand.

Daddy just stared at it. "What the hell are you doing here?"

"Just keeping an eye on your boys."

"That so?"

The two lawmen eyeballed each other for a moment. Ryan and Leo watched, fascinated.

"Well, I got it covered now, Officer."

"I reckon you do." Glenn picked up his hat. Nodded to Ryan, touched Leo's shoulder. "You boys ever find yourself in Quicksilver again, be sure and drop me a line."

"I can't imagine them ever getting up here again." Leo looked at the wound on his ankle.

Glenn put his hat on. "Those are two brave boys you got there, Sheriff." He met both of their eyes. "I'm sure they take after their mother."

"The hell's that supposed to mean?"

"See to your boys, Sheriff." He tipped his cap and stepped into the hallway.

Their father looked momentarily lost, without someone to fight with. His boys braced themselves but were saved by the entrance of Dr. Helfrick and a nurse.

"Howdy, Sheriff."

"Evenin', Doc."

The doctor sat next to Leo, inspected the wound. "Well, the snake got him good but we should be able to fix him up." He turned and gave some technical instructions to the nurse, then turned to their daddy. "We're giving him some antivenin and antibiotics. Should be able to release him tomorrow afternoon."

"Think you can keep from killing this one, Doc?"

The nurse made a shocked noise, a gasp she couldn't quite keep from escaping her lips.

All eyes on the doctor who grimaced and stood. He got very close to their father, almost nose to nose.

The nurse was on the intercom. "Can somebody send Vernon down here?"

"Sheriff, you suffered a terrible loss. So I'll forgive you for saying that once. Say it again. See what happens."

Vernon walked in with curious eyes.

"Think you can keep from killing—"

The doctor's fist slugged their father in his left eye. He staggered back.

"You son of a bitch."

Vernon restrained him. "Easy, Sheriff. Easy does it."

"Get your hands off me, boy."

"Now, you can't hurt the doctor yet. Let him treat your son. Let's all think of the kid, people."

The boys were stunned. They had never seen grownups behave like this. A fistfight? A doctor punching someone? They understood well the urge to strike their father but to see someone, an old man, a professional, act on that impulse altered their view of the world. Leo momentarily forgot the pain in his leg as he looked at Ryan's face, his brother's eyes wide, just the hint of a grin. The doctor looked surprised too, though he didn't look like he wanted to take that swing back any time soon.

Their father relaxed. Vernon let him go, hesitant, hands up, ready to grab him again.

"You fools got a hold of yourselves now?" the nurse said.

Daddy touched his eye tenderly. It would turn black soon. He chuckled. "Didn't think you had it in you, Doc."

"Me neither."

"You know, striking an officer of the law is a serious offense."

"Charge me later. I'm gonna tend to your son."

Daddy nodded. "Thank you."

"You're welcome."

Leo recognized the look on Daddy's face, a rare mood, not angry but sad.

"Guns and snakes," the doctor said. "Two things boys shouldn't play with."

2

2012

It was a land of dust and scrubgrass, sand and rock, punished by the sun, forgotten by God, maybe it was California, but by the time you made it down this busted up road it was hard to remember what country you were in. Might be Mexico, or Hell. Then Sally's Airstream Diner appeared like a mirage out of the desert, shining like a massive bullet.

But it was real.

The old man pulled his rented Chevy sedan into the dirt lot and parked next to a lonely Toyota Tercel. The car engine made angry noises and the air conditioning was just a weak, warm coughing. The old man savored it before turning off the ignition. He picked up a Stetson hat and the pistol underneath it off the cracked leather passenger seat and stepped into the oven of a day.

The early sun, molten red and low on the horizon, seemed close enough to walk to. The old man was still getting used to the sight of it. For thirty years he'd only seen the sun when it had risen above the prison walls that surrounded him. The American Southwest, where a man could see the horizon in every direction, was overwhelming and disorienting in its vastness.

A rattling air conditioner kept the inside of the trailer under a hundred. A bored waitress watched the old man walk slowly to the counter and sit. He put his hat on the stool next to him. She was in her twenties, he guessed. Wore no makeup and didn't need any. Her hair, pulled back in a simple pony-tail, was sun-bleached blonde. An adorable cluster of freckles decorated her nose and cheeks. Her eyes were big and green.

Behind her, a Mexican kid was cooking, bacon and home fries.

"Mornin'," she said.

"Morning." She squinted at him. "We don't get a lot of out-of-towners around here."

"Is that a fact?"

She nodded. "Start you with a coffee?

The thought of coffee made him perspire but he nodded.

"Menu's on the board."

"You Sally?"

She grinned, shook her head, poured his coffee.

The old man nodded as if the last thing had fallen into place. "When's Salvador due in?"

"I expect him, directly."

If she was surprised by the old man's knowledge

of her boss' real name, she didn't show it.

The old man used his napkin to wipe the sweat from his forehead. Maybe late twenties, he thought. Just a touch of world weary in her green eyes. She might have learned a hard lesson or two in her short life. Probably from a man. Twenty-five years ago, the old man had just started to get old. The young lions in the pen had turned on him, as was natural, and his anger had burned even brighter. At the man who put him there.

He hadn't killed anyone in a long time.

That would change today. The more things went well, the surer he became.

This time was different. In prison it had been pure self-defense. Him or them. No kind of choice involved, except the choice to live. Before that, it had been business. He was paid large sums of money to end people's lives. Mostly bad guys who had it coming. Pimps, drug dealers, racketeers. Not always. He could be honest about that. Not everyone he killed went to Hell. He wouldn't go so far as to say he regretted killing a few innocents. It paid just as well. Better on occasion. The world had taught him to accept that bad things happened to good people. So what if he was the bad thing. But he took no pleasure in it. He remained a professional.

Not today.

Today was different.

He would take pleasure in this. Savor it.

Yes, there was money in it, but that wasn't the

point. He would gladly have done this for free. Hell, he would have paid his fee for this target's whereabouts.

Thoughts of how he would do it had given him comfort over the years in prison. Some men imagined women, girlfriends or wives. Late at night, alone in his cell, he imagined murder scenarios. His favorite fantasy, though not practical, was strangulation. Being able to watch Sally's eyes bulge as he fought for oxygen. The old man smiled and looked at his wrinkled, arthritic hands. Couldn't squeeze the life out of a pigeon now.

Oh well.

He could still pull a trigger.

Outside, the rumble of an engine, tires crunching gravel.

"That'd be him," she said.

"Why don't you take a smoke break?"

"I don't smoke."

The old man placed a pack of Marlboros and a book of matches on the counter. "Good time to take it up. What's the cook's name?"

"Angel."

"Take him with you."

The girl waited a moment, then took the cigarettes and left, with Angel in tow, through the kitchen. The old man heard the slap of a screen door.

Salvador's tan skin was leather, his hair lamb's wool. He was heavier, like he'd been living well.

Good. He sighed when he saw the old man.

"Hey, Sal."

"Hey, Teddy."

"You're a hard man to find."

Sal shrugged.

The old man pulled the revolver out of his pants and put it on the counter. Everything felt unreal, dreamlike. Such a long time coming.

"I've often wondered how this would go down."

"Me too."

The waitress' name was Doris. She stood outside, felt the temperature rise with the sun.

"A man will come someday," Sal had said. "Let him do what he has to do."

Even though she expected it, the gunshot made her jump. And the second. And the third.

Angel threw the half-smoked Marlboro she'd given him onto the ground and hopped into his ancient Chevy pickup. The engine coughed to life, sounding like a man who couldn't catch his breath. He looked briefly at the girl, his eyes a question.

She shook her head.

Angel nodded, put the truck in gear, rumbled away.

The old man stepped outside and put his Stetson on. She didn't see a gun. He handed her some cash, tipped his hat. "For the coffee."

A wicked breeze kicked up, furnace-hot. She

turned her back and cupped her hands so she could light the first cigarette she'd smoked in years. Doris waited until the old man's car was out of sight before she went back inside.

3

To get to the Murphy ranch, you took Sidewinder Canyon north out of Oscuro. Followed it as it coiled like a diamondback through the Las Piedras Mountains then straightened out. Occasional mailboxes stood next to long driveways. Homes in the distance occupied by people who liked their space.

The roughly two hundred acres of land was mostly surrounded by a fence. Here by the house it was a handsome white picket fence. A gate usually left open signaled the driveway. The fence turned to barbed wire as it ran all the way to the abandoned mercury mine at the north end of the Murphy property. Between the house and the mine were vast stretches of rocks and sand and mountains. A rugged place full of rugged people.

The house was a long, one-story affair made of white adobe brick. A rust-colored Spanish tile roof covered a stone patio that bordered the front of the house. Two wooden rocking chairs stood sentry on either side of the front door. To the left of the driveway, a single-wide trailer. To the right, a big old wood barn. Their power came from a field of solar panels and three windmills. Sun and wind were in abundance here. Their water came from a well and several huge cisterns that caught the all-too-rare rainwater.

As a child, Leo got used to being alone in the world. After school, when his father was at work and Ryan was at baseball practice, Leo would sometimes pretend he was an astronaut stranded on a deserted planet. Wounded in the crash, he had to limp through this strange, lifeless world.

The phone rang as Leo was trying to coax the feeling back into his snake-bit leg. Nerve damage from when the rattler bit him. Feeling came and went. Occasional shooting pain was another fringe benefit, like an echo of the bite itself, a souvenir. Used to drive his wife nuts when he woke with a scream in his sleep, calling for his brother. Back when his wife was still in the picture.

He hadn't heard from Ryan in a bit either. A difficult man to get a hold of these days. Wanted in the States for a double homicide, he lived for the most part across the border in Mexico. Leo wasn't exactly sure what his brother did over there except that it wasn't legal and likely involved drugs.

He stumbled into the kitchen. The phone continued to ring. This early, his teenage daughter, Cassiopeia, wouldn't get out of bed if the house was on fire. Considering she was suspended from school, she might not get out of bed at all today.

"Leo here."

Mrs. O'Leary, his secretary slash dispatcher said, "Sorry to trouble you at home, Sheriff. But it sounds like all hell's broken loose over at Sally's Diner."

"Define all hell broke loose."

"Some old man shot Sally."

"I guess that qualifies as all hell breaking loose. Christ. This is a bad way to start the day."

"Yes it is."

"Was Doris there?" He couldn't help asking, couldn't keep the extra note of concern out of his voice.

"It was her that called it in. Said some old man came in, ordered coffee, told her and Angel to go outside, then shot Sally."

"Is Sally dead?"

"Dead as Davy Crockett."

"What about the old man? The shooter."

"Drove off east according to your girlfriend."

If only, Leo thought. He'd been sweet on Doris for some time now. But he was taking it slow. Too slow probably. He shook those thoughts out of his head, tried to focus.

"Okay, I'll be there ASAP. Get a hold of Three Js. Tell him to meet me there. Get Becker on the horn too. I want him to take a look at the body."

"He'll be useless this early."

"He'll be more useful than anyone else."

"Roger dodger, Sheriff."

Leo pictured the dead man, Sally. Salvador Compiano was his real name. What Mrs. O'Leary didn't know was that Salvador—aka Sally C—was a federally protected witness relocated from Miami. It was hard to reconcile the amiable old man and his beautiful head of cottony white hair with the list of crimes he'd been granted immunity for in exchange for testimony that put away at least half a dozen mobsters.

Leo dressed in a hurry, cursing that damned snake and his bum leg. He pinned his star on the chest of his khaki uniform shirt. Took a mug of coffee with him on his way to his daddy's trailer.

When he asked his father why he didn't just build an addition or move into a small apartment in town, Jeremiah told him he was born on this land and he planned on dying here. As for building an addition, he didn't want to intrude on Leo's family life. He didn't need much, just a roof over his head, a place to hang his hat.

He'd retired from the force eight years ago and never looked back, or explained his reasons. Leo was unanimously selected to succeed his father by the few dozen citizens who gave a damn. Jeremiah sold off some land to cover his retirement and spent most of his time maintaining the remaining few hundred acres and helping Leo with Cass.

The sun was already glaring meanly at the desert. The trailer was a simple single-wide mounted on a sturdy cement foundation to protect it from the occasional rainstorm. Leo knocked on the door.

"Yeah?"

Leo walked in. The scents of coffee and cigarettes. His dad was at the kitchen table, an Old Gold in his lips, steam rising out of the mug on the table, and a beat-up copy of *The Iliad* open in front of him. A familiar sight from his childhood, Leo almost expected to be asked to go wake his brother before they were late for school. His father was thinner now. When had his hair turned so gray?

"Good morning, Sheriff." Jeremiah Murphy's voice was deep from years of whiskey and cigarettes.

"What's the quote of the day?"

His father examined his son over his reading glasses. *"We men are wretched things."*

Leo nodded. "Sounds about right."

His father wore blue jeans and a denim button down over a ray t-shirt, which was all he ever wore. Brown cowboy boots on his feet, and when he went outside, Leo knew there would be a white cowboy hat on his head. He could have been cast as an aging lawman in a Hollywood Western. Except he had never grown a mustache. Leo didn't think he'd ever seen Jeremiah unshaven. He'd missed his daily shaves so much in Vietnam that he swore when he returned he'd never miss a day. An oath he hadn't broken as far as Leo knew. He kept everything as simple as he could. Inside the trailer there was no clutter. The walls were bare. The living room had a couch and a lazy boy recliner. No television. He did have a radio.

"A bit early in the day to be wearing that star."

"I know it. Some trouble out at Sally's Diner."

Jeremiah frowned. "What kind of trouble?"

"The bad kind. Can you watch the kid for a few hours?"

"You know I can."

"No letting her drive your truck."

"Why?"

"She's suspended from school. I don't want her enjoying it."

"That's a bullshit suspension. That kid called her a ho."

"She broke the kid's nose."

Jeremiah chuckled. "Justice was served. And the boy learned a valuable lesson."

Leo sighed. He wasn't sure who was more stubborn, Cass or his father.

His father stubbed out his cigarette and stood. "And if memory serves, I believe you were no stranger to high school scuffles."

"I don't recall you being too happy with me at the time."

Jeremiah shrugged. "I wasn't too happy with anybody back then."

Sometimes Leo marveled at the change in his father. Ever since Cassiopeia was born, as if a seed of gentleness had been planted and slowly bloomed inside him. Maybe a thought of redemption for mistakes he'd made with his sons.

Leo remembered the tears in Jeremiah's eyes when he first held Cassiopeia as an infant. A few months later Leo was shocked to realize that he couldn't remember the last time he'd seen his daddy take a drink.

When Vikki left Leo, Jeremiah put in for retirement and bought the trailer with money earned from the land he sold. He claimed he'd gone soft and Leo couldn't argue. He had. He'd started seeing the good in people. A dangerous thing in a lawman.

"Thanks, Pops."

Jeremiah said no thanks was needed and walked toward his old house with his Homer tucked under his arm. Then something occurred to him. He turned back to Leo. "Sally's. Isn't that where that girl you're sweet on works?"

Leo scowled. "I'll be back as soon as I can."

"We'll be fine. Maybe she needs a ride home after all this excitement."

"Maybe you could mind your own goddamned business."

"I don't see that happening."

"Me neither."

4

Ryan waited.

In the shade provided by a rocky cliff just north of the border. A steep but quick path behind him back to Mexico. His window was closing. The border patrol unit he'd bought off would avoid the stretch of road in front of him for only another thirty minutes. An hour past his rendezvous time.

Such a simple plan. Borne out of a rare occurrence. Lunch with his brother at a diner. Something about the old timer behind the counter. Nervous eyes. He had the look of someone on the run, somebody being hunted. Ryan did some research. Salvador Compiano. Sally C. An enforcer turned rat about thirty years ago. Put a bunch of guys away. Ryan dug a little deeper and saw that one of the men he stooled on was due for release. A button man named Ted McCarthy.

He arranged a meeting with Don Palermo in Miami. Ryan tried to keep his travel in the States to a minimum and rarely went anywhere but California. But this might be worth it.

Sally C had been a member of one of Palermo's crews and Palermo had sworn vengeance on Sal. There was a standing million-dollar price on his head.

Palermo's home in Coconut Grove was straight out of Scarface. Palm trees, two pools, five garages, and arches everywhere. An armed guard opened the gate and showed him where to park. Once inside, he allowed himself to be patted down. He wasn't carrying. Then he was led to a deck with a view of the bay.

Don Palermo invited him to sit across a table from him. The Don was maybe sixty. Not tall but everything about him was large, his head, his hands, his belly. His tan skin was made darker by the Florida sunshine. His thin gray hair was slicked back. A gold cross on a gold chain rested in the white hair of his chest. He wore a blue sweatsuit.

An expression both skeptical and amused. A booming voice. "So what's the subject?"

"Sally C."

His big eyes narrowed. His smile disappeared. "I'm listening."

"I know where he is."

"Where?"

Ryan decided not to play coy. "California. A little town on the border."

"Salvador Compiano. That motherfucker."

"You got a guy coming out in a couple of weeks."

Don Palermo sipped an espresso. "Teddy McCarthy."

"Maybe let him pull the trigger."

Don Palermo smiled. His teeth were perfect, looked like they could chew through steel. "Not a bad idea." He looked at Ryan like maybe he missed something at first. "Ryan Murphy. Baseball star in high school. War hero in Iraq. Father was a cop. Brother is a cop. You sneak various cargo across the border. They call you the blonde coyote."

"At your service."

He chuckled. "What the hell happened to you?"

Ryan shrugged. "It's hard livin' with the law."

"So why not take care of this yourself? You do it, take the money. Why complicate it with Teddy?"

"I thought Teddy might want to settle a score."

Palermo shook his head. Those perfect chompers must have cost him a fortune. "Or maybe you have an agreement with your brother. Maybe having somebody else pull the trigger honors this agreement."

What was the point of denying it? "Maybe."

"Fair enough. So you'll arrange things in California. A car. A gun. An escape route to Mexico."

"Can do."

"We'll get him there. A fake ID. A plane ticket."

Ryan waited for the last detail. The hard detail.

"My people tell me you're not squeamish. You know how things work."

"I like to think so."

"We need Teddy to disappear after this."

"Of course."

"Do I need to spell it out?"

"No, sir."

"You small town boys. So polite."

"That's the way my mommy raised me, Mr. Palermo."

"This goes well, maybe we do some business in the future."

"I like the sound of that."

"This goes bad..." Palermo shrugged. "Don't let it go bad."

"Understood, sir."

"Good."

They shook on it.

"My man Bill's got something for you. A retainer and a number to keep us informed on."

Ryan knew Bill by reputation. Wicked Bill, they called him. For all the usual reasons. Tall and lanky in a cream-colored suit. Hair cut basic-training short. His right eye was brown and bored. His left eye was blind in the middle of angry burn scars. Ryan had been warned. It was still hard to look at. A lot of rumors about what had happened. Looked like someone had taken a hot iron to his face. Bill handed him an envelope. They didn't speak, just exchanged nods. Ryan was in no rush to ever see him again.

Now Ryan waited.

Above him the sky was a thermonuclear shade of

blue that rippled with heat. The horizon throbbed with the mirage effect, as though the world was melting. He stared north at the land he was born in. At the road that was supposed to have a car on it with the man he was supposed to meet.

He had tried to get away. Went to UCSD on an athletic scholarship. Baseball. A pitcher. But a gambling scandal had cost him his scholarship. To stay in school he'd joined ROTC, the army.

Anything to avoid being in his father's debt.

After school, Iraq.

Letters from his little brother. Packages of coffee and cigarettes and beef jerky. Ryan sent postcards back, short and sweet. *Thanks for the package. Out in 115 days.* He always included how many days he had left. His father sent nothing. Which denied Ryan the pleasure of letters to tear up or packages to throw out.

Daddy never forgave him for Leo's snake bite. The fact he'd saved him counted for nothing. "Never should have been outside," was his take on it.

True enough. Ryan would have liked to ask his dad if he'd ever made any mistakes as a teenager. Or had he been perfect? Had Mom ever forgiven him for anything? But these questions occurred to him years too late, long after the infected scars had scabbed over, too painful to touch.

They communicated as little as possible. Often

using Leo as the conduit, relaying messages back and forth.

In high school, Ryan ran with a rough crowd. Drink hard, play hard, was their motto. There was only so much trouble to get into in Oscuro County. The uncrowded roads were forgiving to drunk drivers. And while Ryan talked tough about girls, he understood the word *no*. Though as the star pitcher of the county, he heard *yes* more often. Those girls responded as much to his vulnerability as they did to his celebrity. They could see the effect his mother's ghost had on him; they knew the story of how he saved his little brother. Let's face it, the pickings were slim in Oscuro County and Ryan Murphy was one ripe apple.

The old man was late. Ryan checked his watch and wondered what had gone wrong. Not that it mattered now. It was time to go. He hefted the backpack with enough food and water for two men and headed back up the hill, toward Mexico.

He should have known. He'd learned it enough times by now. If something could go wrong in Oscuro County, it would. Murphy's law.

5

Leo pulled into the dirt parking lot of Sally's, next to Doris' Tercel. Technically he should call witness protection right away. Salvador had turned state's evidence decades ago, and the feds had let his father know what was up. Some intuition told Leo to hold off. The feds would have a long list of enemies to choose from. No doubt some of the fellas Sally had dimed on were out by now, and angry.

But how did one of them find him? Who tipped them off? His brother seemed the most likely candidate. Leo was in no rush to explain his having a meal with a known fugitive from justice in the presence of a relocated federal witness.

He put his flashing lights on to dissuade any would-be diners. Doris sat on a chair in front of the airstream trailer, smoking. He'd never seen her smoke before. She didn't make eye contact as he approached, just stared toward the horizon, oblivious to him and the blazing heat.

He touched her shoulder. "How you holding up?" He sat next to her.

She turned her pretty face to look at him. "I've been better. I couldn't be in there, alone with…"

"I don't blame you. Coroner'll be here directly. I'm gonna take a look, then I'll need to talk to you for a bit. Okay?"

She nodded, still in a daze. "He knew somebody would come."

"What?"

"He warned me once. I didn't really listen. Said someone would come."

When she teared up and leaned into him, he didn't mind. He savored the feel of her, thin but strong; the smell of her, the smells of breakfast, but underneath, apples and lavender.

"You're okay," he said. "It's all over now."

He squeezed her then stood up. She leaned her elbows on her knees and grinned, wiped her eyes.

"Sorry to go all to pieces like that."

"Nothing to be sorry about. I need to go take a look."

"Okay." She put a hand on his arm. "Thanks."

He put his hand over hers. His mind took a careful inventory of this moment, their most intimate contact so far.

He took his hat off and walked inside. Sal was face up on the floor, his t-shirt more red than white. Blood pooled underneath him. The coppery smell of it competed with the scents from the kitchen. Angel had left the griddle on. The home fries had burned. Pity.

He crouched next to the body. Shot three times. The stomach, the chest, the face. What a mess. It certainly looked personal. Or was made to look that way. A .22 revolver was on the floor, the pooled blood just touching it. He heard two cars pull into the lot. One would be Steven Becker, the local undertaker and coroner. Leo was pretty sure he knew who the other would be.

"He's inside," Doris told them.

Steven Becker and Leo's deputy, Three Js, walked in somber-faced. Becker was a few years younger than Leo's father, sixty-one or two. He liked his booze and he liked his pills. It wasn't uncommon for Leo or Three Js to be summoned to carry him home from the Desert Rose Saloon in the center of town. Other than that, he was a pretty good doctor and a halfway decent man. At the end of the day, he cared. Maybe that was the reason for his habits.

He took a quick sip from the flask he kept tucked in his blazer pocket. "That's a nasty piece of work."

Leo nodded.

Three Js, as always, had little reaction. In his late twenties, he behaved older. He stood maybe five feet nine inches, but his barrel chest and heavily muscled arms made him an imposing presence. He kept his scalp shaved and wore a neat goatee.

"Where's Angel?" His deep voice was surprisingly gentle.

"Bolted. I'm guessing his papers aren't be in order. Might need to track him down."

"Okay, kemosabe. Did she see where the perp went?"

Leo stood. "Let's go find out. Looks pretty cut and dried, Beck. Let us know if you find any surprises."

Beck pulled on gloves as they stepped outside.

"Doris," Leo said. "Which way did the old man go?"

She pointed east.

"Let's take my vehicle," Leo said.

The police lights had done nothing to dissuade the regular morning crowd from entering the parking lot and had probably drawn a few additional civilians who weren't in need of breakfast. Half a dozen vehicles, mostly dusty Ford and Chevy pickups, gathered at the far end of the lot, their drivers poking their heads out of open windows. A few stood out in the heat, smoking and joking with each other. When Leo and Three Js came outside, a man got out of his white Cadillac in a shirt and tie and waved in their direction. Dave Barry was one of two practicing lawyers in town.

"Anyone in need of representation in there, Sheriff?"

Leo shook his head. "Nobody breathing."

"What about the perpetrator?"

Leo remembered that even in grade school, Dave had spoken like this. Always favored ten-cent words.

Dave already had the lowdown or had guessed what had happened.

"I'm sure you learned about discretion and valor at SDSU, Dave."

Dave grinned his lawyer grin. "Must have skipped that class."

"We find anyone in need of representation, we'll be sure he has your number, counselor."

"Much obliged." Dave tipped his white Stetson and walked back to the crowd of ranchers and laborers who would eventually go downtown to La Cocina or go to work hungry. But not before filling up here on as much gossip as they could.

6

1965

Teddy McCarthy was fifteen the first time he killed a man.

He lived in the Lindenwood neighborhood of Queens with his mother. She was a pretty, tired lady. Since his father had left, she'd been working as many shifts as she could at the Lindenwood Diner. She was usually gone when he woke for school and often not back until dinner time, when she'd lug whatever food she could finagle home from work.

It was a Saturday. His mother was taking the day off and they were going to the World's Fair in Flushing. Finally. Finally see those towers up close, taste the Belgian waffles all his friends had been talking about. In the midst of this anticipation, they heard a knock at the door.

He was a huge man, well over six feet, his legs and arms bulged against the fabric of his suit. Frank Nulli liked his henchmen well dressed. He was a collector, Bobby Bennevento, went by Double

B. Sent to strong-arm his mother. Teddy's father had left them with a gang of gambling debts before skipping town. Left her holding the bag.

"Mr. Bennevento, I'm sorry but I'm not going to pay that lowlife's bills anymore."

Double B chuckled and shook his head. His voice was deep and hoarse, he smelled like cigarettes. "Tell you what, pretty lady. I'll waive the vig for a week. For you, for your troubles. Next week, the meter starts to tick again and I'll clear up my books, one way or another."

Teddy saw the vein in her temple throb the way it did after he broke Mrs. Carmichael's window playing stick ball.

"You married a loser. It happens. We all have to pay for our mistakes sooner or later."

Over forty years ago, Teddy still remembers the surge of adrenaline. At fifteen he was a hundred fifty pounds of jumpy rage. Mad at the world. And now this fat bully came into their home and disrespected his mother.

No.

He went to the hall closet. Grabbed the big hammer.

Teddy waited until the man was out on the street. Walking to his next shakedown.

Double B never saw it coming.

A perfect swing caught him right in the temple. Teddy felt an electric buzz course through him. A lightness in his lungs, in his limbs, as he swung again and again. Righteous. That was the word.

The next thing he was aware of was his mother at the door of their building. A dreary November day. A light, cold rain.

"Come inside, Teddy. Clean yourself up." Like he'd skinned his knee falling off his bike.

He looked at the man, at his smashed in head and face.

"Come inside, Teddy."

He still held the hammer. She led him to the sink. Helped him wash the blood off his hands, off the hammer. The smells of soap and blood coalesced.

"Change your shirt."

Scarlet stains on his chest. Teddy nodded and did as he was told. He marveled at his mother's calm. No yelling, no tears. She put on her coat, told him to get his. They walked outside and hailed a cab. He'd never been in a taxi before. She gave the driver a name. "Carmine's." The back seat still had the smell of a bus or a subway, a riot of odors from various passengers all mixed with the driver's Camel cigarettes. Teddy grabbed his thighs to keep his hands from shaking.

The cab went south to Howard Beach. Apartment buildings gave way to single-family homes closer to the water. Seagulls flew circles in the gray sky. Later Teddy would learn that this was around the time mob bosses started moving to Rockwood Park.

Again and again, the sound of the hammer on

skull in his head.

They stopped in front of a brick restaurant. A red neon sign in the front window read Carmine's. She thanked and paid the driver. Teddy followed her inside.

A fat man with olive skin and dark curly hair smoked a cigar at a square table. He recognized his mother, probably from the diner. "Julia?"

She nodded. Her hands squeezed each other. "Is he in?"

He put his cigar in an ashtray. "Hang on." He stood and walked to a back room. Low murmurs. He returned and nodded. "Let me take your coat."

"Thanks." She unbuttoned it and handed it to him.

He nodded to Teddy to do the same.

"What's your name, kid?"

"Teddy."

"Okay, Teddy, I'm Anthony. Why don't you have a seat while your mom talks to the man."

He must've looked panicked because his mother said, "It's okay, Teddy. I'll be right back."

As Anthony led his mother to the back of the restaurant, he hollered, "Carmine, get the kid some bread and a Coke."

An older man with a head of salt-and-pepper hair and a white mustache, Carmine held a basket of garlic bread in his left hand, a Coke in his right, and a cigarette in his lips. He placed the food in front of Teddy.

He ate.

All of it.

Then licked the garlicky butter off his fingers. Washed it down with a sip of Coke. Alone, he pictured the hammer hitting bone. The blood. The body of Double B, so still, on the sidewalk in front of his apartment building. He closed his eyes, beholding true dark now. Teddy searched his soul for regret. Found none.

After a while, Anthony returned. Alone. Motioned for Teddy to stand. He followed him to a dim room at the end of a narrow hallway. His mother was there. Not scared exactly, shook up. She sat off to the side. At a wooden table in the middle of the room, a man in a suit sat. The man motioned for Teddy to sit opposite him.

The man's mouth smiled. His eyes did not. Nor did they blink.

"Hello, Teddy."

Something in the man's eyes and his voice scared him. His voice trembled. "Hi."

"Do you know who I am?"

Teddy shook his head.

The man nodded. "My name is Benito Gallo."

Teddy's heart fluttered, his breathing stalled. He knew that name. You heard it whispered low, under people's breaths. When men ended up dead in alleys or in cars. Men shot in the back of the head or with their throat slit.

"Your mother tells me there was a problem today.

With one of my men. Bobby Bennevento." He raised his eyebrows. "Well?"

Teddy nodded.

"What happened?"

He looked at his mother who nodded once. Then he took a breath. "I hit him with a hammer."

"And?"

He swallowed, said, "And I killed him." He forced himself to keep his eyes on Benito Gallo's.

After a moment, Benito Gallo nodded. "It's a terrible thing, killing a man. Isn't it?"

Teddy nodded.

"But there are worse things." He nodded his head toward Teddy's mother. "Like something happening to your mother. Right?"

"Yes."

"Good. So you did what you did today for your mother?"

"Yes."

A grin on Benito's mouth. His eyes were doing math, some grim calculus. "What I need to know is, can you do it for me?"

2012

Such a nice, simple plan, Teddy thought to himself. And it had all gone so smooth. The rental car was there waiting at the airport in his false name. The gun, the .22 under the seat and loaded, as promised.

And Salvador had been where he was supposed to be and had died, just like he was supposed to. Killing a man hadn't felt that good in a long time. Maybe since Double B.

All shot to shit now.

Maybe he'd driven too fast, not used to these desert roads. Maybe the tire'd been too worn, due to bust. Maybe Teddy was just cursed. Whatever the cause, the tire had blown with no spare available.

He was good and fucked.

The sun climbed. So did the mercury. Felt like God was holding a magnifying glass between him and the sun, trying to burn him like an ant. Christ, he was thirsty. The taste of Sal's lousy coffee clung to his teeth, caught in his throat. He wanted to spit but couldn't spare the water.

Damn, but that was a lot of blue above him. Not one fucking cloud, not a hint of rain. He might just die out here. What a bone job. Far overhead, the silhouettes of carrion crows circled, riding thermals. He extended his right middle finger at them.

He was grateful for his Stetson. Bought to help him blend in, it was his only source of relief. He tried to picture himself on a map. A map. He looked in the glove box. A map of California. Bingo. He found the town. A dot in the middle of nothing. He traced the road he was on with his finger. The border didn't seem far away on the map but looking south at the barren wasteland beneath a merciless sun, he doubted he'd get too far. He listened to the sound of wind, felt it push the heat over him.

Then he heard a car approaching. A brand-new Ford Explorer. White with *Oscuro County Police* written on the side. Perfect. He leaned against the hood of his miserable rental car.

Ain't that a bitch.

7

"Where's Daddy?"

"Out chasing bad guys."

She nodded, moved to the pantry. She lived on cereal and potatoes. Fourteen years old. How could that be, Jeremiah thought. He remembered Cassiopeia's birth like it was yesterday. Now she was tall, thin, and long-legged, her light brown hair wild like a lion's mane. She filled a bowl with Frosted Mini Wheats, poured milk over them.

There was already a small plate on the kitchen table with her medicine on it. Jeremiah didn't know what it was. Didn't like that she had to take it.

She ate. It was not a pretty sight. She didn't close her mouth when she chewed, head low over the bowl, humming something to herself. Jeremiah pictured kids at her school, the popular ones, the mean ones, making fun of her. He imagined himself slapping their faces, breaking their noses, shattering their jaws.

If she'd been born in an earlier time, she'd probably have been thought to be possessed by demons, maybe burned at the stake as a witch.

With her mouth full of cereal and milk, Cassiopeia squinted at him. "What are you looking at?"

"A hungry girl."

The answer seemed to please her. He knew better than to criticize or comment on her habits, or worse, try to correct them. Last time he tried that he had to duck a full bowl hurled at his head. It startled him to see the echo of his own awful temper in this fierce girl. Only made him love her more.

He remembered his Homer. *Rage—Goddess sing the rage of Peleus' son, Achilles, murderous, doomed, that cost the Achaeans countless losses, hurling down to the House of Death so many sturdy souls.* She had some killer in her, no doubt. But then, that was a Murphy family trait.

"So what are we doing today?"

"The north fence needs mending."

Cassiopeia grinned. "Can I drive?"

"I reckon. Just don't tell your daddy."

"Target practice?"

He chuckled. "I reckon."

Jeremiah packed his ancient Chevy with a cooler filled with ice and water. Another cooler with sandwiches and pickles and a six pack of beer. He packed a shotgun, a .38, and a .22 pistol in the bed with a shovel and a pick and six new fence posts. His .45 revolver was on his hip, just like when he was sheriff.

She was champing at the bit, hands squeezed into fists on the wheel. "Let's go, Papa."

He hopped in on the passenger side.

She turned the key, goosed the gas pedal a bit, and the engine came to reluctant life. The truck in gear, Cass jumped on the gas, knocking Jeremiah's head back even though he knew it was coming.

"Goddammit."

Her giggles as they bumped over the rough desert made him happier than just about anything.

A few of the posts on a northern section of fence had rotted and the barbed wire was nearly touching the ground. It was simple work, but not easy. First he dug the old posts out. Clouds rimmed the edge of the horizon. Otherwise the only ingredients of the deep blue sky were a furious sun and a ghostly half moon. Granddaughter and grandfather both wore hats and sunglasses against the sun but still felt the need to squint.

Cass helped him pull the old posts out when the time came. They stacked them next to the truck. Jeremiah worked up a powerful thirst. The ice water tasted so good it stunned him. He wiped the sweat off his face with a red handkerchief then put it back in his pocket. They took the new posts out of the bed of the truck and slid them, one at a time, into the ground like a sword in its scabbard. She held the posts straight while he packed the earth tight around them.

In his younger days, Jeremiah drank a beer for

every post he replaced. Now he poured a full bottle on the ground around them, as if he was watering them. Then he placed the empty bottle on top of the post. The smell of the beer conjured old memories, bad memories.

"Why don't you drink the beer?"

He smiled. "I drank enough beer in my day to last the both of us the rest of our lives."

She pursed her lips, shook her head. "Did you used to do this with my daddy?"

"Once in a while." He bent and pointed at one of the old posts. "See there?"

She knelt and touched the bullet holes in the wood. "You think that's from my daddy?"

"Or your uncle."

Leo had been a good shot, and he'd devoted himself to becoming better. But Ryan was a natural. Once he had the hang of it, he didn't miss often. As good on the draw as he was standing still and aiming. Some people just had the knack.

Once the six bottles were placed, Jeremiah went to fetch the firearms. "What are we starting with?"

With a mischievous smile, she pointed at the pistol on his belt.

He chuckled. "That thing'll knock your skinny ass on the ground. Let's work our way up. Start with this."

He handed her the .22.

She rolled her eyes. Then she checked the chamber and the magazine. He admired the way she handled the weapon, her seriousness and focus. He stood back and watched her line up the shot. The first bullet hit wood but the second shattered the bottle she aimed at. Then she pivoted right at the waist, arms locked in place, hands steady, she fired at the post to her right, the second bottle burst into pieces.

A natural. Like her uncle.

"Gimme a bigger gun."

8

"Looks like our boy," Three Js said.

"I reckon."

The old man's sedan tilted toward a flat tire. The man leaned against the car. He looked out of place, uncomfortable in the heat, in the new hat, blinking against the fierce desert daylight.

"He look like a killer to you, Sheriff?"

Leo chuckled. "You know what a killer looks like, Deputy?"

They pulled up behind the vehicle.

"Watch yourself," Leo said.

Three Js unfastened his holster.

"Sometimes these old codgers are crafty."

They stepped out of the Explorer, wincing at the heat.

"Car trouble?" Leo said.

"You must be some sort of detective." A northern accent, maybe New York. He sounded like somebody out of a Scorsese movie.

"Sheriff."

"Don't suppose you'd have any water you could

56

spare, Sheriff?"

Leo grinned. "It does get a little hot in these parts this time of year."

"A bit."

"I'm gonna guess that you know what I mean when I say, assume the position."

The old man spit, then turned and placed his hands on the hood, spread his legs. "Could do with a cigarette too."

With a hand on the butt of his service revolver, Leo nodded to Three Js who frisked the old man.

"Be gentle, amigo."

Three Js couldn't quite keep from smiling. When he was done and found no weapon, he stepped back and shook his head at Leo.

"You two mind telling me what this is about? Did I miss a stop sign somewhere?"

The old man's calm was disarming. "Do you mind if I take a look in your vehicle, sir?"

"Not exactly mine. Just a rental. Help yourselves."

There wasn't much to find. The name on the rental agreement matched the name on his New York state driver's license. Virgil Smith. The trunk was empty.

"What brings you to these parts, Mr. Smith?"

"Please, call me Virgil. I was going to do some camping."

"Camping?"

"Maybe a little hiking. I hear your national park

is really something."

Leo looked at the old man's sneakers. "Where's your gear?"

"Oh, I figured they'd have everything I need."

Leo had to admire the old man's cajones. "You stop anywhere recently? Maybe for a bite to eat?"

"I wish I had. You mean there's a place that serves food out here? I could sure use a bite."

"Okay, Mr. Smith. We're gonna take you into custody."

"For what?"

"Well somebody shot and killed the proprietor of that diner. Witness places a gentleman that matches your description at the scene of the crime."

Three Js had his cuffs out.

"Are those really necessary?"

"Shut up before I cuff your ankles too," Leo said. "Stop me if you've heard this one before. You have the right to remain silent."

9

Ryan couldn't put it off any longer. It was time to make the call.

Wicked Bill answered on the first ring. His hoarse, scratchy voice said, "Is it done?"

"The first part."

"One old man down. One to go, then."

"Second old man's in custody."

Wicked Bill let silence do some work for him.

Ryan waited, flexed his jaw, rubbed his eyes.

"So clean it up, cowboy. I'm on a plane in an hour. Clean it up before I get there and I'll buy you a drink."

"You already bought a ticket?"

"I bought it right after you left. Hoped I wouldn't need it."

"And if it isn't cleaned up?"

"I clean it myself."

Now Ryan let the silence expand.

"Understood?" Bill said.

"Understood."

Ryan dropped the burner phone to the ground

and stepped on it with the heel of his boot. Two ways to clean this. Remove the perpetrator or remove the witnesses. Maybe a third way. Eliminate all of the above.

He looked around at the pathetic town of San Polvo, Mexico. A few tourist trap shops, a saloon with a cathouse upstairs. A place frozen in time. Other than electricity and running water it was the same town Panza was rumored to have visited before he disappeared into the mountains. Ryan doubted the old outlaw ever made it this far west but it was always a place for bandits and desperadoes to gather supplies.

Now it was also a place where Mexicans and Central Americans looking to get into El Norte collected, like debris left on the beach after a storm. Nobody wound up in San Polvo on purpose. They got blown here like tumbleweeds. Broke and desperate, easy prey for the coyotes who prowled the dirt streets. Men who promised an easy trip north for a price, cash or trade.

Ryan walked into the saloon, La Taza Vacía, to the sound of horns and guitars coming from the jukebox. He sat at his usual stool and nodded to the bartender, Pedro, who fetched his usual, a shot of tequila and a Pacifico.

"Bad day?"

"Aren't they all?"

Pedro shrugged. "They all the same. I give you that." His English was improving.

Ryan held up his tequila in a toast and downed it. "That's better."

Pedro's eyes turned sly. "Was some people in earlier. Asking about El Coyote Rubio. Looking to get north."

El Coyote Rubio. The blonde coyote. Ryan's Mexican alias. He moved cargo both ways across the border. Drugs and people north, guns south. A small-scale operation, he didn't want too much attention.

"Not today, Pedro."

Pedro nodded, began cleaning glasses. Poured another tequila. He took commissions from Ryan and the other coyotes in town. "I like to go to you first, amigo."

Ryan smiled and handed him a folded twenty-dollar bill. "Gracias."

How long, he wondered, until Wicked Bill arrived? It would be so much easier if his brother were not the sheriff right now. But usually that was not the case. For most of Ryan's business it was a very good thing that his little brother was the sheriff of Oscuro County.

10

2004

Leo was not looking forward to going home.

He was stalling, having a drink at the Desert Rose, even though he knew the later he got home, the longer his wife and daughter were alone together, the worse it might be. Sawdust on the floor. Pacifico on tap. Haggard on the jukebox. Probably wasn't a song recorded before 1980 available.

Marcos Chavez had owned the Rose for as long as Leo could remember. A squat, chubby man with a big head topped by slicked back gray hair and a face dominated by a bushy white mustache. He was cleaning glasses.

"Your father used to do the same thing."

"What's that?"

"Come in here for a few pops when he didn't want to go home. My business took a dip when he quit drinking."

"Sorry to hear that."

Marcos shook his head. "All for the good, Sheriff.

All for the good. How is he?"

"He's well."

"Tell him Marcos said hi."

"I'll do that."

Their daughter had always been a handful. Cass was a bad sleeper who bawled until she vomited when they put her in the crib at night. When she was one, she would leap out of the crib onto the floor like some sort of kamikaze pilot. In school she was a holy terror from day one when her kindergarten teacher, Mrs. Youngs, called to inform them that Cass had bitten her hand when she tried to take away her doll.

Now Cass was seven and her second grade teacher, Mrs. Gifford, a sweet, fat old lady, was near the end of her rope.

Leo and his wife, Vikki, and Cass had spent the day before at a neuropsychologist's office in Quicksilver. Cass was put through rounds of tests and interviews. Leo and Vikki sat in the waiting room, tense, not speaking.

The two of them had met privately with the doctor before the testing began. Leo winced when Vikki said, "I just want her to be normal."

A small, sad smile on the doctor's face. "Well, Mrs. Murphy, I've seen a lot of patients over the years, and normal is the rarest diagnosis there is."

"What about happy?" Leo said.

The doctor pursed his lips. "I'll tell you something a lot of people either don't know or don't believe. If your child is on the spectrum, I find that they have more potential for happiness than most." He held up a finger. "If they are understood and provisions are made. If not, if their condition is ignored or marginalized, as it often is, then, sadly, these patients can cut themselves off from social interaction. That's what we want to avoid. Let's talk in a few hours."

It was the first time either of them had heard the word "spectrum" used that way. It would not be the last.

Later, after the tests, Leo wondered if the doctor ever tired of the looks on parents' faces, the desperate need there. Leo watched Vikki's expression as the doctor informed them that, in his opinion, their daughter's behavior put her on the spectrum, high-functioning, but still there. Leo resented the tears in his wife's eyes.

"Autism?" she said.

The doctor cleared his throat. "People hear autism and they think of *Rainman*. Or a nonverbal individual. That's not your daughter."

"What do we do?" Leo hated having to ask.

"We can try some medication. She exhibits signs of ADHD, and there are things we can prescribe for that. To provide focus and lower anxiety."

The image he couldn't get out of his head was a picture his daughter had drawn. She was asked to reproduce a picture of a house, a simple image full of squares and triangles and rectangles. Cass' drawing looked as though the original drawing had melted. Rather than divide the house into separate shapes, Cass had started with the outline, trying to draw that first, then filled in the details, ending up with a mess of curved lines and rounded corners. If he hadn't seen the original, he doubted he could have guessed what she was attempting to draw; it knocked the wind out of him.

"Now imagine," the doctor said, "how she sees a school assignment. How difficult it would be for her to separate a large project into different sections. How easy it would be for Cass to get overwhelmed."

Leo couldn't take his eyes off the messy illustration.

"Counseling would be helpful. And there are some groups she could join, group therapy sessions with similar kids."

"What about school?"

"She will be designated special ed. I will draft a letter with provisions she needs. Now, I don't know what your school's resources are…"

Not much, Leo thought.

"She does have one big advantage over some other kids in her situation."

"What's that?" Vikki asked.

"She is incredibly bright. We did some IQ testing as part of this. She's off the charts. That's what makes her so hard to diagnose."

When they came back into the waiting room, Cass was building a castle in the corner with some blocks. "Are we done yet?"

They went to Dairy Queen after. Cass devoured an Oreo Blizzard. Leo and Vikki picked at their dishes of ice cream which soon turned to soup. Leo would think of something to say, then decide against it when he saw the defeated look on Vikki's face. She stared off at the horizon like a prisoner looks out the bars of their cell.

He'd seen that look before—prisoners counting off the mistakes and bad decisions that had led them to that lonely cage in the middle of nowhere.

"It's going to be okay."

Still staring toward the far sky. "Is it?"

"Yes."

"I need a drink."

"We'll get you fixed up at home."

She gave him a hard look. "I don't feel like waiting that long, Leo. We're getting her something at the pharmacy. Let's get me something at the liquor store."

She drank a six pack of Lone Star on the drive home, didn't speak to Leo or Cass. Just stared west out the passenger window, for escape routes.

They drove with Cass' window down. She loved the air against her face, liked to stick her arm out and move her hand up and down like a fish swimming upstream or a bird flying into the wind. Leo watched her in the rearview mirror and savored the look of contentment on her face. He made a vow to himself to do what he had to do to keep that expression on her face.

It was impossible to drive any considerable distance in Oscuro County without feeling small, insect-like. The lonely, cracked roads and sun-faded signs might have been the ruins of some ancient civilization swallowed by the hungry desert. Out here everything man made was fighting a losing battle.

"Did they figure out what was wrong with me?" Cass asked all of a sudden.

Had she been wondering that since they left the doctor's office? He adjusted the rearview mirror, met her nervous eyes. "There's nothing wrong with you, kid."

She snorted. "That's not what everybody else says."

"Who says?" He felt his fingernails dig into his palms as he strangled the steering wheel.

Cass' eyes darted, for just a second, toward her mother. Then she looked back out her window. "Never mind."

Vikki finished her fifth beer. He heard the cap twisting off her sixth beer over the sound of blood pounding in his ears.

"There is not a goddamned, fucking thing wrong with you, Cass. No matter what anybody says."

"Anybody?" Another furtive glance at Vikki.

"Anybody."

Her expression turned thoughtful; tried to process this new information. "Why do I need medicine? Am I sick?"

"We'll see if the medicine helps."

"Helps what?"

"Helps you not drive your teachers crazy."

Cass smiled. "Maybe Mrs. Gifford needs medicine."

"Well, it's either give you medicine or give everybody else medicine."

A giggle.

"Okay?" he asked.

"Okay, Daddy."

When they got home, Vikki switched to vodka. On the rocks.

It was a ramshackle house not far from his family ranch. Lots of open space, not a lot of neighbors, none within sight. Leo walked out onto the patio with a cold Pacifico. Christ, it tasted good. Half a sun paused on the horizon then sank quickly, the sky a study in purple. When the color had left the sky, he went back inside.

Cass was on the couch watching television.

"Did you have dinner?"

She pointed to an empty bowl on the coffee table. "SpaghettiOs."

"It's about bed time, kid."

"Can I finish my show?"

"Yeah."

In the kitchen, he sat across from Vikki and her vodka.

"Need a drink?"

He raised his half-full beer. "Got one."

Her eyes were unfocused, her face red from drink. "It's hard sometimes, being married to a saint."

"I'm no saint."

"Always say the right thing, always do the right thing. It's like I married fucking Gary Cooper."

"What do you want me to do?"

"Aren't you scared? Aren't you angry?"

"Sure."

She scoffed. "You sure look it. When's the last time you were scared?"

Leo looked outside at the darkness, remembered the sound of a rattle, the terror in his gut. He shivered.

"What?"

"Nothing."

She took a long taste. "Right. The strong, silent type."

It helped, sometimes, to remember when they were kids. He recalled her eyes when he'd shown her where the rattler had bit him. Wide and scared, as her fingers touched his skin. A warm feeling where she touched him, an echo of that heat in his chest for being the object of her fascination. A long time since anything had fascinated her. Much longer since he had fascinated her.

"Look, all we can do is all we can do, Vikki."

"What if that's not enough?"

"Enough for what?"

Her eyes puddled. She muscled down another sip, nearly knocked over her glass. The dim light and the booze turned her blurry and ugly. A sad sight. What did she want from him? Something, he thought. An urge to slap her fought with an urge to embrace her. Would either help? Would she remember either tomorrow when her head cleared?

She closed her eyes and held her temple, stayed like that for a good minute or two, her other hand on the glass.

"Daddy, my show's over."

Vikki opened her eyes. "Still here? Better go. Your princess needs you."

He stood and left the room.

The walls of his daughter's bedroom were pink. Toy horses and ponies in every scale littered the floor. Pictures of horses on the walls and on her bed sheets: morgans, palominos, mustangs. Even her pajamas had horses on them.

"Will you read me a story?"

"If you get ready fast."

"What should we read?"

She handed him a slim hardcover book. *The Girl Who Loved Wild Horses* by Paul Goble.

"Again?"

She shrugged, smiled.

He opened it and started to read. He lay next to her on the bed so she could see the pictures. He read in an intimate whisper as if the story was a secret he was sharing with her. He had read it so many times he could almost recite it by memory. When he was finished and the girl had disappeared to join the wild horses, he turned to find Cass asleep.

The scent of her as he kissed her on the forehead, then turned off her lamp. He left her door open. Moved quietly down the hall. Vikki was slumped on the couch, empty glass clutched in her hand. He gently removed it and set it on the table. He found a blanket and spread it over her. Her breathing was heavy, vodka fumes snarled out of her mouth.

He rubbed his face. It didn't need to be easy. Did it have to be so hard?

His secret pack of Marlboros was stashed in the cabinet above the refrigerator. That and a fresh beer before he walked outside and lit up.

He'd been drawn to it ever since that night he'd been bitten, before that probably. He was in love with the Oscuro County sky at night. The big blackness, lousy with stars. Drawn to it like some are drawn to the edge of the ocean. It made him feel small. Made his problems seem small. For a moment. He looked back toward the house, its lights seemed part of the sky, another constellation, light years away.

11

Leo couldn't ask his father for advice. Not about girls. Not about Vikki. So he turned to Ryan.

"Victoria Messino? That mean little thing? She'll eat you for breakfast, little bro."

Leo pictured her. The pretty face with the stern expression. Lips that rarely smiled, unless her sneer counted. He wanted to get past her defenses. He was sure, once she let her guard down, there would be tenderness and substance.

His injury had been his first experience of her soft side. He wanted more.

"You want to know how to get her interested?"

Leo nodded.

Ryan grinned. "Don't be such a damned boy scout."

"What do you mean?"

"Knock off the puppy dog eyes. The creepy looks during class. Ignore her. Or at least let her think you're ignoring her."

"But how do I get her to notice me?"

Ryan held up a finger. "Make it impossible not to notice you."

"How?"

"Make everybody notice you."

"I don't get it."

"Get into trouble, dude. Mouth off to your teachers. Get into a fight. You want a girl like Victoria Messino, that's what it's gonna take."

Soon after that conversation, there was a junior high dance. The first dance for Leo's class. They were held in the school gymnasium. Leo wore one of Ryan's old Izod polo shirts with the alligator on the chest.

She had on a light blue dress, strapless, that showed off her tan shoulders and her shapely legs. He tried his best to know where she was without staring.

Leo wasn't the only one who noticed Vikki's icy beauty. The other boys lost patience with her withheld affection. They got angry.

A commotion in the back of the gym. The Police on the speakers. "Every Little Thing She Does Is Magic." Kevin Dunphy, red-faced. Leo would find out later she'd just slapped him.

"You little cockteasing bitch," Kevin shouted over the music.

A riot of blood pumped to Leo's extremities as he stepped into the circle surrounding Kevin and Vikki. Kevin was a year older. Brown hair parted in the middle and feathered back over his ears and the collar of his shirt. A jowly moon face. He had a few inches and about ten soft pounds on Leo.

"Take it easy, Kevin."

"Fuck off, Hopalong." A nickname that had stuck with him after getting bit by the snake. Even though he didn't limp that much anymore.

A buzz in Leo's chest as he stepped close to Kevin and shoved him.

Leo glanced around but Vikki had slipped into the crowd. He turned his attention to the pissed off eighth grader charging toward him, mayhem in his blue eyes.

More advice from his brother came to him. *You get in a brawl with a bigger dude than you, don't let him line up his shots. He comes at you, you come at him, fast, before he has time to react.*

Leo made himself move forward. Surprise on Kevin's face.

Hit him in the sternum. Knock the wind out of him.

Kevin's eyes went wide. The breath came coughing out of his lungs.

Hit first and hit last.

Leo hit him in the head, landed a right on his ear. Did it again.

Then grown-up arms had Leo by the waist. Another teacher had Kevin in a headlock, saying, "Easy boys. Easy does it."

The music still playing. "Stairway to Heaven."

74

Our shadows taller than our souls. The last song at every dance.

The teachers had smirks on their faces. Boys will be boys.

"Get off of me," Kevin hollered.

Leo didn't struggle. So Mr. Erardi let him go, but stayed between the boys. "That's enough for tonight, boys."

"You're dead, Murphy. Fucking cheap-shot artist. You're a dead man," Kevin said and stormed off.

Leo couldn't help a small swell of pride in his chest.

Then the song ended and the lights came on, revealing everyone's true faces, hair wild, cheeks red from dancing, mascara running from crying, a Cinderella-at-midnight feel. The girls fled the bright lights like mice, scurried outside.

He followed the crowd. His friends buzzed around him. The talk on everyone's lips was the fight between Leo Murphy and Kevin Dunphy. Leo's friends swaggered outside because there was no doubt who had won. "Did you see Dunphy's face?" people said.

Make everybody notice you, Ryan said.

Mission accomplished.

Outside, the cool desert breeze brought relief after the stuffy gymnasium. Leo was still braced for an ambush from Kevin but he saw no sign of him. His hand was smarting from hitting Kevin's head. He was tired now that the adrenaline rush had worn off.

A line of cars driven by parents and older siblings formed at the curb. Dramas came to an end as new couples and just-broken-up couples separated for the night. "You're making a huge mistake," Becky Sherman shouted at Scott Johnson then rushed to her parents' car.

A hand on Leo's shoulder.

Vikki had a nervous smile on her face. "Hey."

"Hey."

"Thanks. For back there with Kevin."

Now that he had her attention he had no idea how to keep it. "He's an asshole."

She giggled. Could everyone else see this? The pretty girl focused only on him. Laughing and smiling just for him.

Leo didn't realize he was rubbing his right hand until she took it in hers. "Does it hurt?"

It did. "Nah."

"Looks like your knuckles are swelling."

"I guess."

She looked closer, bent her head to inspect his injury, tucked her light brown hair behind her ear. Planted a tender kiss on his center knuckle. She let his hand go. He had to keep it from floating over his head.

"Better put some ice on that."

He could only stand there, tongue-tied and stupid.

She looked over his shoulder. "My ride's here. I guess I'll see you on Monday."

He had to clear his throat. "I guess so."

She held his gaze for a moment, a smirk on her lips, one eyebrow arched, then turned and walked to her mother's peach Ford Pinto. Her mother was trouble according to most of Oscuro. Beautiful but starting to show some wear. Divorced and on the prowl, people said. She was either too much or too little. Smoked too much, drank too much, swore too much. Wore too little, worked too little. Too much makeup. Too little morals. She was one of the few adults he knew that Leo could picture having sex.

The car door opened and the dome light revealed Vikki's mom. Puffing on a Parliament with her too-bright lips. "Is that you, Leo Murphy?"

He waved.

"You be sure and say hi to your daddy for me." She winked at him, made his heart stutter a beat.

"Yes, ma'am."

Vikki and her mom pulled away.

"What the hell was that?" his friend Richie Henry asked.

Leo held up his hands. It was something.

Ryan Murphy closed his eyes and shook his head when Leo told him the story as he iced his fist in a bowl.

"What?"

Ryan sighed. Captain of the baseball team. A senior. College scouts came to watch when he pitched. A different pretty girl on his arm every week. Leo could think of no better authority on navigating adolescence.

"Well, that's one way to do it."

"I did what you told me to do. And it worked."

"Just be careful. She likes you fighting for her. She'll make you do it again."

Leo didn't care. He'd beat up half the school for her attention.

"And remember. No googly eyes in class. Make her come to you."

He tried. But his fascination had doubled. In his head, The Police sang "Every Little Thing She Does Is Magic" and he couldn't keep his eyes off her. She couldn't help but notice. Her polite smiles at his attention turned to bored, irritated sighs. He'd blown it. So close.

Then it was summer.

Ryan was going to college in the fall. Leo's friends all played sports. Leo worked with Three Js' dad and his father on the ranch. Mended fences, dug trenches. The hard work under the vast blue sky kept his mind busy. Not seeing Vikki every day helped him not to think of her.

He saw her on the first day of eighth grade, in the hallway, his friend Rusty Perlman's meaty arm around her shoulder. She giggled at him the way she once giggled at Leo.

That's why they call them crushes.

He avoided her, ignored her. If she made a joke in his presence he was careful not to laugh. Without meaning to, he followed his brother's advice.

For two years.

Three.

A blur of classes he didn't care about. Why bother? He'd just follow his father into the sheriff's department. Get a cruiser, a pistol. As close to a cowboy as you could get these days.

1988

Another dance. Leo was sixteen now, a junior in high school. He drove his dad's old pickup with a bunch of friends in the back. A few beers, a bottle of something stronger snuck from somebody's parents. Allison Lawson riding shotgun. A skinny blonde with pretty blue eyes and a waist Leo could nearly reach around with his hands.

The air inside the hot gymnasium was a whirlwind of scents. Obsession by Calvin Klein, Beautiful by Estee Lauder, Love's Baby Soft. Hair held in place by Aqua Net or LA Looks. When you came close to groups of boys, the stink of Polo by Ralph Lauren and Drakkar Noir. The stench of teen angst.

By this time Leo had become an expert at ignoring Vikki. That ship had sailed, he told himself. That night, she was impossible not to notice. Her hair up off her tan neck, the low-cut black dress that hugged her curves and stopped way before her knees.

Damn, was the word on every boy's lips as she passed.

Then the shouting started.

"Just stay the fuck away from me, Rusty!"

Rusty, on wobbly feet, clearly tipsy, mumbled something. Lurched toward her. A few girls had come to Vikki's defense. Rusty shoved his way past them. Shoved a little too hard.

That feeling of deja vu in Leo's gut. He didn't remember how he got there. Between Rusty and Vikki.

Rusty said, "Mind your business, Murphy."

"Take a walk, Rusty. Cool off."

Jon Bon Jovi sang, *Take my hand, we'll make it I swear*.

Rusty wavered. The peppermint schnapps he'd had before the dance made it tough to decide what to do. Part of him must have felt the same deja vu as Leo. Like he'd been thrown into a situation he recognized but in a different role. He just needed Vikki to listen to him, though. Just needed to plead his case to him.

Leo didn't move. He was aware of Vikki behind him, touching his back. No way out of this now.

Neither boy wanted to fight the other. But a pretty girl can tip the balance of these situations. Drunk sixteen-year-olds can lose perspective in a hurry.

"Vikki, I just want to talk." Rusty on the edge of

tears.

"We're through talking, Rusty. Go home."

Leo watched as Rusty's sadness turned to rage. Here we go, he thought.

The music changed. The Bangles. "Walk Like an Egyptian."

A switchblade in Rusty's hand. A girl screamed. Not Vikki.

Leo didn't wait.

He pounced. Caught Rusty's blade hand between his forearms and twisted. Used his weight to pull Rusty to the ground, Leo on top. The blade fell to the floor. Leo kicked it away and stood, just as two teachers showed up.

"What's going on here?" Mrs. Spencer asked.

"Rusty fell. Just trying to help him up." Leo held his hand out.

Rusty shoved it away. Stood up on unsteady legs.

"Mr. Perlman, you feeling okay?"

Rusty thought about it. Nodded.

"You been drinking, young man?"

"No, ma'am."

"I hope not. Miss Messino, everything okay?"

"Yes, ma'am."

"I hope it is."

In the crowd surrounding them, Leo saw Allison Lawson's disappointed blue eyes. She turned and walked away.

Rusty walked away too, weaved through bodies

walking like Egyptians. The teacher at the door told him once he left, he couldn't come back.

"Good," Rusty said and pushed the door open.

"Come on," Vikki took his hand.

She led him to a door in the back of the gym that led to an equipment room. In the back of the room another door opened to the south hallway of the school lit only by red exit signs.

"I need some peace and quiet."

She let go of his hand. They walked past rows of lockers. She stopped at hers. Spun the combination. Opened it. Books piled on the bottom. Up top was a small salon. Aussie Mega Spray, a tin of something called Lip Lickers, and a bottle with an exclamation point on it. Leo leaned his back against the next locker. She reached behind the beauty products and came out with a silver flask.

"Here's mud on your eye." She took a small sip then offered it to Leo.

He took a belt. Whiskey. He handed it back.

"Why was Allison Lawson looking at me like she wanted me dead?"

"We kind of came together."

Vikki nodded. Took another sip. "What am I gonna do with you, Leo Murphy?"

Whatever you like, he thought, then shrugged.

"You keep beating up my dance dates." She squinted at him. "What's a girl to think?"

"Sorry about that."

"Are you?"

"Not exactly. Maybe you should pick better dates."

A grin.

"Allison's a pretty girl."

"She's okay."

"She's probably missing you."

"So what?"

"So you'd rather stay here with me?" She moved a step closer.

His heart was too big for his chest.

"You sure, Leo Murphy? I'll just break your heart."

He couldn't think of anything better than having his heart broken by Victoria Messino.

She moved right in front of him. "Last chance to run away."

He leaned down. The scent of her a complicated mix of flowery perfume, hairspray, and whiskey.

They kissed.

Lips closed, then open, tongues tasting each other. After a few minutes they paused.

She smiled. "That was nice."

He nodded.

She sighed. "This is such a mistake."

He was afraid to speak. Afraid he'd say something stupid.

"Why'd you have to be so cute?"

"You're not so bad yourself."

"Thanks. I guess."

"You're welcome."

She giggled. "Kiss me again why don't you?"

"Okay."

She pressed tighter to him this time. Good Lord. Is this really happening?

After a while she said, "What time is it?"

"I have no idea."

He didn't know what hit him. A fist to his temple dropped him to the floor.

"You bitch."

"Rusty, you're drunk."

"So what. I'll be sober tomorrow. You'll still be a bitch."

Rusty grabbed her by the wrist.

"Let me go, Rusty." Her voice cracked. Tears in the corners of her eyes.

"So this is your new man? Hopalong Murphy."

Leo got to his feet. "Let her go, Rusty."

"Or what?"

"Come find out."

"Rusty, just go away. Go sleep it off," she said.

Rusty backhanded her with his right fist.

Leo's brain came unwound. He was on Rusty, fists on his face, his eyes, his nose, the dull thud of flesh hitting flesh over and over again.

Vikki was shouting at him, but she sounded far away. Hard to hear her over the much closer, much sweeter sound of Rusty's head against a locker.

"Stop," she was saying. Her hands were pulling at his arms.

He stopped. Suddenly back from his beserker rage. Finally aware of what Rusty looked like.

"Go get help," he said between deep breaths.

She hesitated, afraid to leave him alone with Rusty.

"I'm done. Go get help."

She kicked off her high heels and ran barefoot toward the music. Wham. "Wake Me Up Before You Go Go."

Leo's fists echoed with pain like just rung bells. He opened and closed them. It hurt.

Rusty bled, eyes shut, mumbling to himself. His nose was surely broken, right eye swollen shut.

Leo sighed. "Fuck." He pulled Rusty into a sitting position against Vikki's locker. Dents where he'd bounced Rusty's head off it.

A commotion of footsteps and teachers' voices came toward him.

"Here we go," Leo said.

As the faculty tended to the unconscious Rusty, Vikki knelt next to Leo. "You okay?"

"Are you?" He touched her face where Rusty had slapped it.

"I'm fine. That was scary."

Leo tried to recall how it felt for him. Not scary. For the first time, he thought he might understand his father's joy at punishing someone who truly deserved it. "Sorry. I don't like people hitting you."

"That makes two of us."

"Somebody call the police," Mrs. Spencer said.

Leo winced. "That's not gonna go well."

His father was there before long. His familiar

heavy gait down the school hallway. The music had stopped. The dance was over. Jeremiah froze when he saw Leo. His cop eyes went from his son, to Vikki, to Rusty. He pursed his lips and nodded. A young deputy with him.

"Go meet Becker out front. Get him in here ASAP."

Everyone was quiet, watching. They could all hear Jeremiah's knees creak as he squatted in front of Rusty. He frowned. Put his palm on Rusty's head and pulled an eyelid up with his thumb. Rusty's bloodshot eye rolled back, his head jerked.

Jeremiah turned to his son. "Your handiwork?"

"Yes, sir."

"Rusty was out of control, Sheriff. He was drunk. He slapped me."

Jeremiah stood. "I'm wondering what the three of you were doing in this hallway. All by your lonesome."

Becker and the deputy pushed a gurney down the hallway.

"I needed something out of my locker."

"Pretty girl, your best bet right now is to shut up. Unless you want me to search for what you might have needed in your locker."

Becker stopped the gurney in front of Rusty. His eyes widened when he turned and saw Leo. He winked at the boy, then took inventory of Rusty's injuries.

"Busted nose. Maybe a concussion. Tough to tell because he's so inebriated." He felt Rusty's head, checked his arms, legs, and ribs for further damage. "Don't see any more breaks. Plenty of contusions."

"So he'll live?"

Becker nodded. "Don't like the look of that eye." He waved to the deputy. "Benny, help me get him on here." He lowered the gurney so it was just above the floor. They took a hold of Rusty. "Count of three. One. Two. Three."

"Four," Rusty said as they lifted him.

Once he was strapped in, they wheeled him away. Then it was just Leo and Vikki and Jeremiah.

Leo wasn't too surprised when the slap came. A sharp smack to the temple. Leo didn't protest, just rubbed the spot where he'd been hit. Vikki seemed too shocked to speak.

"You sober enough to drive?"

Leo nodded.

"Straight the fuck home," Jeremiah said. "Miss Messino, I'll get you home. Don't worry. Your mother's taken a ride or two in a state vehicle in her time.

Beneath a sky fat with stars, Leo drove home, replaying the night's events in his head. The fighting, the kissing. *What am I going to do with you, Leo Murphy?* What indeed. The memory of her lips on his stirred butterflies in his gut. What was that if not love? Now she was in the back of his dad's cruiser. Rusty Perlman was in the hospital. What a fucking night.

Ryan was in the kitchen, drinking milk out of

the carton, when Leo walked inside. "You get any-where with that Allison girl?"

"Not exactly."

Ryan rifled through the fridge. "Christ, there's nothing in here. What do you two live on?"

Leo shrugged.

"What's with you? You looked spooked."

"There was a little scuffle."

"Again? Man, what is it with you and dances? Tell me it wasn't over Vikki."

"I'd like to tell you that but I'd be lying."

Ryan shook his head. "Let me see your hands."

Leo was suddenly aware of how sore they were.

"You need to ice these." Ryan filled two bags with ice. "Sit over here."

Leo sat in the recliner. He put his arms on the arms of the recliner. Ryan placed a cold bag on each hand.

"Okay, little brother. Tell me about it."

Ryan listened. A perfect audience. He laughed at the funny parts, he winced at the painful parts, he winked whenever Vikki's name came up.

"He pulled a knife? On you?"

Leo nodded.

"She sure can pick 'em."

"How long until you ship out?"

When Ryan had gotten himself thrown off the baseball team—Leo never knew the specifics but figured a girl was involved—he'd opted for ROTC rather than come home. He'd be doing four years in the army.

"Next week. Friday."

"That soon?"

"Gonna miss me?" He flicked Leo's earlobe.

"Hell no."

Ryan chuckled. "Good. I'm sure the old man won't either."

"He will. He just won't say it."

"That's him in a nutshell."

Leo readjusted the ice bags. His hands throbbed but felt better.

"So was she a good kisser?"

Leo blushed at the memory. "Yup."

"I heard her mom was too."

"Screw you."

"What?"

Before long, Jeremiah parked his cruiser in the driveway. The sound of his cowboy boots on the front steps. He nodded at his sons on his way to the kitchen. A can of Lone Star popped open. A glass was filled with ice and Jim Beam.

He carried his beverages into the family room. Sat in his leather chair. Looked at each of them. Took a sip of beer.

"How are the hands?"

"He'll live," Ryan said.

Jeremiah took a sip of Beam. Grimaced. "I'm just gonna say this the one time. You do what you want. That girl is bad news. Just like her mom."

"Okay, Dad."

Jeremiah held up his hand. "Hey, I get it. She's beautiful. And you could have a real good time with her. I'm just telling you, she ain't a girl to help you through tough times. And there's always gonna be tough times."

"I need a beer," Ryan said.

"Get one for your brother too."

Ryan shot a surprised look at his father, then looked at Leo and got two beers out of the fridge.

"Get another one for me too."

It was the first time Leo ever drank in front of his father. They all sipped without comment.

"My life sure as hell didn't turn out like I pictured." Not much to say to that.

"How's Rusty?" Leo asked.

"You fucked him up pretty good. Busted nose. Maybe a rib or two. Lost a tooth."

Ryan giggled. "Nice work, Rocky."

"Don't worry, you'll be getting the bill."

"That's bullshit. He came at me. He hit Vikki."

"There's defending yourself and then there's what you did." Jeremiah drained his bourbon. "Best you learn the difference. Medical bills will still be cheaper than a lawyer if he presses charges—and you still might pay the medical bills."

It took Leo two years to pay off those bills. He became an indentured servant to his father. Two years of fixing fences and repairing the barn. A lot of time spent out under a big blue sky, feeling small and alone. Thinking about what Vikki might let him do to her at night in the cab of the pickup—what she might do to him.

High school was a series of breakups and makeups. The weekends were a blur of football or baseball games, Vikki taking sips from her flask and passing it to him. The end of the night down a lonely road fumbling with her clothes in the truck, getting a little further each time.

There were other girls in between. He lost his virginity to Patty Cooper on a crisp October night in his junior year in the cool grass of Indian Park. A fact he would deny to Vikki when they got back together around Christmas. Just in time for him to have to buy her a gift.

The circumstances of their engagement were a small town cliché. She got pregnant. Leo begged his father for his mother's ring. Jeremiah refused. Leo stole it anyway, out of its box in the top drawer of her old dresser, still full of her unmentionables.

"When your marriage goes tits up," Jeremiah said, "I expect that ring back."

Leo became a deputy for his father. Signed up to do his basic training at Clark Training Center in Riverside, California.

Vikki miscarried two months later.

Leo drove her to the hospital in his Crown Vic, lights flashing, siren wailing like he wanted to. Later he'd have to take a hose and bucket of soapy water to clean out the back seat.

Just the two of them in the hospital room in Quicksilver. She was in the bed. He was in a chair. Still kids themselves.

After a long silence, she said, "You know what the worst thing is?"

"What's the worst thing?"

She looked at the door before leaning toward him and whispering, "I'm relieved."

"What?"

"We aren't ready. Are we? Are you?"

"I guess not." He'd started to picture it though. Holding a child. Tucking it in at night. Feeding, changing. But he did have to admit the thought of a child terrified him at times.

"I think we've still got some growing up to do."

"I suppose we do."

"Could you do me a favor?"

"Anything."

"Get me a fucking drink."

"I could arrange that."

"Well arrange it then. And tomorrow get me the hell out of here."

"Yes, ma'am."

"Leo?"

"Yeah?"

"Tell me it's going to be okay."

He stood and walked over to the bed. Took her hand. "It's going to be okay." He kissed her hand.

He'd believed it at the time.

12

2004

In the morning he woke early, alone. Vikki was still passed out on the couch. He made a pot of coffee while she snored and left before either girl was awake.

Dawn was an explosion of red and blue behind a flock of cottony clouds. The town was deserted. He parked his Crown Vic in front of the station.

Three Js was asleep in his chair, feet on the desk, head tilted forward. When Leo closed the door, he stirred awake.

"Quiet night?"

Three Js rubbed his eyes, smiled. "Yup. Lorraine called to say her dog ran away."

"Been a good week since we heard from her." Lorraine's dog had died years ago. At ninety-two, her memory wasn't what it once was. She generally called every few days.

"I told her we'd put an APB out for it."

"Sounds like a good use of resources. Let's hope

for a quiet day."

"How'd you make out at the doctor?"

Leo thought of how to answer. "Good, I think. They had some ideas. Some medicine."

"More doctors?"

"Probably."

Three Js made a sour face, a look Leo knew well. An expression that said, you white people do what you like. "How's Vikki?"

"Why don't you go home and get some sleep?"

"That bad?"

"Not good."

"Lo siento, amigo."

"S'okay. We'll figure it out."

Now Three Js would go home to his wife, Maricruz, and his daughter, Juanita. He would make them breakfast and drive Juanita to school. Maybe he would come back and make love to Maricruz. Leo hoped he would. He hoped they were happy. That someone was.

The town still hadn't come to life when his brother came through the front door and said, "Good morning, Sheriff."

Leo couldn't keep a grin off his face. He noticed a surge in his chest. His big brother was home. "Morning. What's the occasion?"

Ryan glanced around, made sure they were alone. "What? I need an occasion to visit my little brother?"

"You were just in the neighborhood?"

"Sort of."

"You want a cup of joe?"

"Sure."

Ryan's dirty blonde hair was longish, a few days' worth of beard on his face. He looked thin, his jeans and his tan western button down hung loose on him. The buckle on his belt was gold and black, a knife with two arrows crossed behind it. The Latin phrase, *De oppresso liber,* on the bottom. The motto of the US Army Special Forces. He sat on the chair in front of Leo's desk, took his straw hat and aviator shades off, put them on the desk, and crossed his black snakeskin boots in front of him.

"How are Vikki and Cass?"

"Good. They'd love to see you."

Ryan sipped his coffee. "Wish I had time."

Leo doubted that very much.

"How the hell do you stay here? What's the appeal? The emptiness, the desolation, the sand?"

They'd had this conversation before. Leo let him talk.

"Have you ever even seen the ocean? Waves taller than you, white caps. The sound is hypnotic."

"I've heard."

"You've heard."

"That's why you came by? Risked getting picked up by some overzealous border patrol cop with a good memory for wanted posters to tell me I should go to the ocean?"

Ryan shrugged. "You should." He chuckled and drank more coffee. "How's the leg?"

"Okay. Comes and goes. Like always."

"Look, an opportunity has come up."

Leo looked dubious. "An opportunity?"

"Don't say it like that."

"Like what?"

"Like Dad would say it."

"Fine. An opportunity."

"I know you don't know what I do for a living."

"Hard to know what you don't tell me."

"Like I said. Lately I've been moving some cargo for some amigos south of the border."

"Maybe it's better if I don't know."

"Maybe."

"But..."

"But there's this opportunity."

"An opportunity moving cargo. Most of it's moved near El Paso or Los Angeles. Near large cities. More traffic, easier to hide maybe."

"But..."

"But maybe there's an opportunity somewhere else."

"Somewhere not as heavily populated."

"You always were quick on the uptake, little brother."

"What do you need from me?"

"Sins of omission, hermanito. Sins of omission. I won't ask you to do anything, just maybe not do anything on occasion."

"Such as?"

"Such as, don't look here on this night. Don't be there on that day."

"Cargo, huh?"

"Not asking questions would be another of these sins of omission."

"There's a question people are always asking me."

"What's that?"

"What's in it for me?"

"The only question that really matters."

"What's the answer?"

"What do you make a year?"

Leo thought. "Twenty-five big ones. But I'm up for a bump next year."

"Christ, that's depressing. So let's say one hundred big ones."

"What?"

"I'm not in the mood to haggle. You heard me right. A one with five zeros. You don't like it, no problem, no hard feelings. I move on to the next small town. Find a sheriff with less scruples than you."

Leo was only half listening, thinking about Cass. Remembering his vow to keep her happy. Money might help. Might help a lot. "Okay."

"Okay?"

Hard to say which brother was more surprised.

* * *

Now Leo was not looking forward to going home.

Leo drank his beer. Marcos stacked clean mugs behind the bar.

"Want to talk about it?"

"No."

Marcos winked. "Neither did your dad. Want another?"

"No."

"Time to go home, I think. See the wife and daughter."

Their money problems were over. Doctor's appointments. Private school. Medicine. Whatever Cass needed, he could provide. It only cost him his soul. A price he was willing to pay for her. The only question, should he tell Vikki about it?

He drove home, the Crown Vic bounced on the unpaved road, a cloud of dust in his wake, the occasional sharp clang of a loose stone banging the undercarriage. Sensations so familiar he barely noticed them. Kenny Rogers on the radio, "Lucille."

Their other car, the shitbox Subaru, was missing from the driveway. The sense that it had been gone a while. The kitchen light was on.

Dozens of reasons why the car could be gone. They might be shopping, out to dinner. He racked his memory for some school event. A concert? A play? Nothing came to mind.

Something made him approach quietly. Like he was arriving at a crime scene. He shut his car door gently, took light steps to the kitchen door. He kept an eye on the window. No movement. Inside, his brain took snapshots. A cereal bowl on the table with only a bit of pink-colored milk in it, a spoon inside. A half full cup of apple juice. Cass' usual after school snack. He realized he had a hand on his gun.

Did they leave in a hurry?

The sink was empty, plates and dishes left to dry in the rack next to it. Two coffee cups. The pan Vikki used to fry her eggs. He looked outside the window above the sink. Same view he'd known all his life, just from a different angle. A vast openness, an uneven landscape populated by stone and creosote bushes bordered on the horizon by the Oscuro Mountains. A land of desperadoes.

"Hi, Daddy."

He couldn't help jerking. Then he turned and saw his daughter smiling at him. "Hi, darlin'. You here all alone?"

She looked at the floor. "Yup."

"Where's Mommy?"

Still looking at the floor. "She didn't say."

"She didn't say?"

A tear formed in the corner of her eye and rolled down her cheek. "She just said she was leaving."

"Did she say when she was coming back?"

She wouldn't meet his eyes. He waited, in no rush for an answer. More tears now, her lips trembled, her nose ran. He found a napkin and bent to wipe her face.

"She said she wasn't coming back."

Her face found his chest. He held her tight while she bawled. She better not come back, he thought as he rocked Cass back and forth. He didn't know what to say so he didn't say anything for a while. He thought of the future, and felt scared.

13

2012

The old man exercised his right to remain silent on the ride back to the diner. Virgil Smith from New Jersey, if his license was to be believed.

"You don't look like a Virgil, Virgil," Leo said.

The old man smiled. "I get that a lot."

Once he was in the back seat, Virgil, or whatever his name was, clammed up.

Leo listed their tasks aloud. "Need to call the feds, let 'em know they lost a witness. Got to get Virgil's car towed to the station. Get the old man printed, find out who the hell he really is."

"Who you think he is?"

Leo eyed the old man in the mirror. "I'm betting he had a score to settle. Short odds say he did time. Even money, Sal's testimony put him there."

"How'd he find him?"

"That's the jackpot question." He turned to the old man. "Don't s'pose you'd like to answer it, would you?"

The old man looked out the window, a Mona Lisa grin on his face.

"Didn't think so."

"We're missing an eyewitness."

"Yes, we are. Think you can handle booking this, old codger?"

Three Js nodded.

"I'll take Doris' statement. After you book Virgil here, see if you can track down Angel."

"Bueno." He chuckled.

"What?"

"Maybe give the señorita an escort home."

"You too, amigo?"

"Hey, we're all just looking after your interests, Sheriff."

"That so?"

"Sí, señor."

When they got back to Sal's diner, Three Js and Leo stepped out of the vehicle. They each aimed a resentful glance at the sun. An ambulance had arrived with some men to help Becker with the body.

Doris sat on the bench outside, still too spooked, Leo figured, to go back inside. She was smoking a cigarette. The policemen tipped their hats as they went back inside. Becker had a large bag next to Sal's body.

"Any surprises?" Leo said.

Becker shook his head. "Just what it looks like."

It looked like a cold-blooded murder. Probably an old score being settled.

"Thanks, Beck."

"That's the job, Leo."

They transferred the old man to Three Js' vehicle.

"See you back at the ranch, Sheriff."

"See you there, Deputy."

Three Js shut the door and started the engine.

The old man cleared his throat. "She told me she didn't smoke."

"What?"

"The chick. The waitress. She said she didn't smoke."

"Was this before or after you shot Sal?"

The old man laughed.

"Something funny?"

"You get as old as me, Deputy, you'll find a lot of things funny that other folks don't."

Three Js put his cruiser in gear. "I don't doubt it."

14

2002

Angel's story was not a new one.

Narcos were taking over small towns up and down the coast of the Gulf of California near his hometown. Seizing land and local power, killing whoever stood in their way. His mother suggested it: Go north, find a home. He said, no. Many times. But the stories from nearby towns kept coming, got bloodier. Finally, Angel said, okay.

He bought a bus ticket to Hermosillo. He was eighteen. All the money his family had made off tourists traveling to Tiburon Island, some tortillas and rice and water in a bag he carried over his shoulder. When he looked back on that dumb kid, he chuckled at his own foolishness. He had never been more than a mile inland, never been to a city. Never been to a place of business where he hadn't known the owner his whole life.

The bus headed east through a wasteland of sand and rock before giving way to neat squares and rectangles of farm land. Acres and acres. Angel wondered where the water could come from to sustain it. Fields of cotton and wheat and potatoes. He lost track. It all became a blur of crops. How could there be so many people to need so much food?

Then in the distance he saw more buildings than he'd ever seen in his life. Houses packed together, with no yards. Three- and four- and five-story structures. They passed a massive hospital.

"Es Hermosillo?" he asked the old man sitting next to him.

The old man laughed until he coughed. Then laughed again. Not yet, he explained.

More farm land. Mountains to the left, tall and white.

Angel dozed.

The old man nudged him awake. He pointed a gnarled finger at the window. "Es Hermosillo."

It was overwhelming. The sprawl of a million Mexicans. Angel's eyes bulged. So much to see. Too much. He looked out the windows across the aisle. Ahead, in the front windows, the city grew, straight up. He blinked. His breath caught.

The old man chuckled again. "Donde vas, amigo?"

"Mexicali."

And from there? The old man wondered aloud.

Angel hesitated.

"El Norte? Los Estados Unidos?"

Angel sighed. "Sí."

The old man pursed his lips, squinted at Angel.

Told him of a town called San Polvo. Close to Mexicali. Go there. Look for a man they call El Coyote Rubio. In a bar called La Taza Vacía.

"El Coyote Rubio?"

"Sí."

By the time they reached the bus station on the eastern edge of the city, Angel's mind was overwhelmed at the crowds. Of people, of buildings, of everything. The old man took pity on him. Led him to the ticket gate and even stood with him until the ticket to Mexicali was in Angel's hand. He showed him where the bus would leave from.

Angel asked if it was a long trip.

The old man sighed. "Muy largo." He told him to get something to eat and to bring some water. Then he turned and left. The only person Angel knew out of the whole city. Angel felt more alone than he ever had by himself on a boat in the middle of the Gulf of California. Or walking the empty desert that surrounded his hometown.

He ate two tacos from a street vendor which only made him homesick for his mother's cooking.

In his peasant shirt and worn sandals he knew he looked like a bumbling indio. He was. He felt the contempt in people's rolling eyes when they saw him.

He had no watch. Could not see the sun to judge what time it was. He waited who knew how long for the bus. A crowd gathered around him. Finally a bus driver arrived to open the door and collect their tickets.

He took a window seat near the back. An old lady sat next to him, so short her feet did not touch the floor of the bus when she sat down. Her white hair was pulled tight into a bun on top of her head. Her skin resembled a well-worn saddle, worn and wrinkled. Out of a large bag in her lap she pulled yarn and needles and started knitting what looked like a blanket. She made no acknowledgment of Angel.

The bus crawled through streets choked with traffic. The driver wasn't shy about using his horn to get his way. Every time he honked, Angel's neighbor muttered a curse under her breath.

Eventually they found their way to the 15 north. Miles of grasslands and green mountains to the east. Miles of sand and ivory-colored mountains to the west. Angel knew the desert lasted all the way to the coast. He pictured his home there. Would he ever see it again? He doubted it.

Angel tried to sleep but the occasional pothole would jar him awake just as he nodded off. The old lady would swear quietly to herself every time.

He was tempted to ask where she was headed, what her plans were. But he didn't want to have to answer the same questions.

In Santa Ana, the bus stopped at a station. Some got off, some stayed on. Angel and the old lady kept their seats. She was making progress with her blanket.

Before long they were moving again.

Route 2 west into a vast desert wasteland that seemed like it would never end. And it didn't. For a long time. Hours and hours of nothing. Hours. Not even many other vehicles on the road to break up the monotony.

Watching the fat sun on its slow descent, the enormity of what Angel was attempting struck him. The world was much bigger than he had realized. Sonora was a land full of strangers. Strangers who eyed this Seri kid with skeptical eyes. As he traveled through this empty land, Angel felt very, very small.

A purple and pink sunset cheered him for a moment.

Then an inky, dangerous dark. The headlights of the bus seemed inadequate to this impenetrable Mexican evening, as if the shadows had defeated the light.

The bus kept moving.

The old lady kept knitting.

The night grew darker.

Until, far away, a quivering light, tiny as a firefly. Slowly, it grew until it blossomed into the lights of a city. San Luis Río Colorado. Angel will not be so happy to see the gates of Heaven as he was to see those lights. Rolling hills made the lights vanish for a time, then reappear, bigger, closer. He kept his eyes forward as the lights multiplied and the city appeared as if summoned by the force of his need.

The old lady did not even glance toward it. He envied her focus on her task. Wondered who this blanket was for. A grandchild, no doubt. Maybe a great grandchild.

They passed into the city limits, left the desert behind them. Manmade lights everywhere. Comforted by this, Angel fell into a deep sleep.

He was asleep when they reached Mexicali. Didn't stir as the bus came to a stop at the station. As the passengers all got off at the last stop. The driver almost didn't realize he was there. Angel woke when the man touched his shoulder. His eyes blinked open. He'd had a dream that he ran away from home.

Not a dream.

"Última parada, amigo."

Angel nodded. He was covered by the old lady's blanket. He nearly wept at the gesture. He folded it, put it in his bag, then exited the bus. Apologized to the driver who only chuckled and waved.

The bus station was quiet, almost abandoned.

A woman at a desk yawned. He asked her for a map. San Polvo was not on it, but she pointed to an empty spot where it should be. She took a pen and drew a star there.

"Cuantas kilómetros?"

She bit her lower lip. "Diez o doce mas o menos."

He thanked her. Bought a bottle of water and a bag of chips from a vending machine.

After three or four kilometers of walking the streetlights grew sparse. He found a nice grassy spot a hundred yards from the road under a copse of chihuahua oaks. Used his bag for a pillow and wrapped himself in his new blanket.

For the first time in his life, Angel fell asleep without the sound of the ocean in his ears. He heard it in his dreams.

At first light he rose and set out east toward the dawn. When the sun crested the horizon it lifted his spirits for a few miles. But the further he walked the more the desert reasserted itself. The green drained from the landscape. Sand and rocks began to dominate the views. The sun climbed. Grew brighter. Hotter. Angel took his straw hat out of his bag, lowered the brim against the sun. He saw a sign for San Polvo. By noon he reached it.

A small, dusty town. The church steeple was the tallest building in sight. Angel took it as a good omen, made a sign of the cross.

It was a town out of an old Western. Even Main Street was a dirt road. The saloon was easy to spot because of the winging doors in front. La Taza Vacía. Angel stepped inside. The name suited it. Other than the bartender and three patrons on stools at the bar, it was empty. And dim. Not much cooler for the lack of sun. The smell of stale beer and stale dreams, the air thick with disappointment.

Angel didn't know if his entrance had stopped the conversation or if they had been sitting in silence.

To the right, two old men with shaggy gray hair and beards and wrinkled leather skin nursed tequilas and watched Angel approach with indifferent expressions.

The bartender's face was skeptical. Eyes that had seen it all. A heavy set man with a few white patches in his goatee. He stacked mugs from a drying rack, which showed off his Popeye forearms and bear paw hands.

The man in front of the bartender did not turn to look at Angel. Slender, with longish blonde hair, he shuffled a deck of cards and started a game of solitaire.

"Hola," the bartender said.

"Hola."

"Que necesitas?"

"Cerveza?"

The bartender nodded. Filled one of his mugs from a tap, placed it in front of Angel.

"Gracias." Angel took a sip. Christ it was good. Gulped some more.

The bartender made small talk. Where was Angel from? Where was he going? Angel was vague. South. North. Neither answer surprised the bartender.

The thought of where he was from made him think of his mother. He took a small wallet sized photo from his pocket. She smiled at him in faded colors. His memory made the colors true. Her skin darker. Her teeth whiter.

"Buscando para alguien."

This caused the bartender's eyes to rise. "Quien?"

"Se llama el coyote rubio."

The old men's whispered conversation stopped.

They eyed Angel now with open curiosity.

So did the bartender. "El coyote rubio?"

"Sí."

The man next to him didn't look up from his cards when he asked, "Quien es la chica?"

"Como?"

"La chica. Quien es?" The only girl in the bar was the one in Angel's hand. He fought an urge to put the picture back in his pocket. Keep her to himself.

"Es mi madre."

"Claro." Of course. The man moved the ace of hearts. "La extrañas?"

Did he miss her? "Claro."

The blonde man turned to look at Angel for the first time. Thin, but wiry, with cold blue eyes above a week's worth of stubble. It had to be the face of el coyote rubio.

"Quieres mi consejo?"

Angel would take any advice offered. "Sí."

"Vete a casa."

Angel shook his head. There was no going home. It was not safe for him. He told the blonde man.

"Seguro," the man said. Safe. His face looked amused. "You think it's safe up there?"

Angel shrugged.

The man held his hand out. "Give me the picture."

Angel hesitated.

The man curled his fingers back and forth.

Angel handed him the picture.

The man held it gently by the corners. After a

112

minute he seemed to reach a decision. He handed the picture back. "Do you have any money?"

"Some."

"Are you afraid of the dark?"

2012

Angel kept a getaway bag in his truck at all times with some clothes, some cash, a Spanish bible, and a picture of his mother, Lidia. Always ready to run. Now the time had come. He pointed his rusty old pickup south and made for the border. Nothing in his rattrap apartment that he would miss—except maybe the chicken thighs he had marinating in a spicy citrus sauce. Oh well. He knew better than to go there—or anywhere the police might look for him.

The sheriff might not know where to look but Three Js would. Three Js might even think to tip the border patrol off. Angel hoped they'd be too distracted by the murder to worry about one insignificant wetback. It wasn't like he pulled the trigger.

The closest border crossing was in Pachuco, twenty miles away. He patted the dash of his truck, prayed that she wouldn't break down on the way. She wasn't used to such long trips. He called his truck Jolene.

She made it through customs. Border patrol didn't try too hard to keep Mexicans out of Mexico. They gave Jolene a thorough inspection, but there was nothing to find. Once he was through the checkpoints and into the desolate no man's land on the other side, she started to tremble. He went nice and slow.

He'd hoped never to return but in his heart he knew he would. In optimistic moments he imagined gaining citizenship and sending for his wife. Now this crime left him with no job and the police certainly looking for him.

Ryan had put the word out to his man at the border. When the man noticed Angel's unmistakable antique Ford, he let Ryan know. Ryan headed west in his black Jeep Wrangler. Before long he spotted the old truck puttering along. No cars ahead. None behind. Perfect.

He pulled on a pair of gloves then put the sawed-off shotgun in his lap, rolled his window down. He stomped the gas pedal and swooped alongside the right of the pickup, aimed at the front right tire and fired. Two pops, the rifle and the tire, and the truck shuddered off the road.

Ryan stayed next to the truck. Threw the sawed-off onto the passenger seat and picked up his 9 mm. When the truck came to a halt he was out of his car, pistol aimed at the driver.

Angel's eyes were wide and scared. He saw Ryan approach and stammered, "Por favor."

Two more pops.

Ryan slipped a pair of gloves on then grabbed the bag on the seat next to Angel. He emptied it of the clothes and the bible. Still no cars on the road. Then he found the picture of the pretty Mexican girl.

He had to move. But he sat. Remembered the last time he'd seen it. Remembered the kid who'd handed it to him. Ryan had taken him north in one of his tunnels. The boy had been scared but brave. A good combination.

He bent and placed the photo in Angel's shirt pocket. "Lo siento, señora."

Hopped back in the Jeep and headed back toward San Polvo.

He tried to feel the relief of a task accomplished. Reminded himself that the world was made up of predators and prey, hunters and hunted, big bad wolves and little red riding hoods. He knew there was no point in mourning the hard ways of the world. There was a big bad wolf on his way to town and Ryan needed to keep from getting eaten.

But still regret gnawed at him, and he had a familiar thought: What the fuck had he become?

15

As Angel was tasting oxygen for the last time, Three Js took Coyote Canyon north to Old Highway 80, called the Old Road by the locals. Oscuro was a few miles west. The police station was in the heart of town, a heart with a pretty faint pulse. Downtown was about fifty shabby homes four square blocks north of Main Street. The main drag was made up of the police station, the post office, a laundromat, the restaurant La Cocina, the Desert Rose Saloon, a general store, a lawyer's office, a dentist's office, and Becker's office. Terra-cotta-roofed awnings provided what shade they could above the sidewalks. There was not a traffic or streetlight in town or for miles beyond.

Three Js pulled in front of the police station. Across the street was the Oscuro Community Park with its dusty fields and the public library. Beyond the park far to the south you could just see the tall wall that marked the Mexican border. The old man let out a sigh. Three Js didn't need to be a mind reader to translate his prisoner's thoughts. *So close.*

He allowed Three Js to lead him inside without a fuss.

Mrs. O'Leary had seen it all over the years. According to legend, her husband had been a federal marshal years ago and died in the line of duty. Beside herself with grief, she'd begged Jeremiah Murphy for a job, anything to help put bad men away. Or words to that effect. Three Js would have liked to ask her the real story but she wasn't a woman that invited personal questions. She dressed like a librarian, in long skirts and buttoned-up blouses. Her gray hair was pulled back into a tight bun and wire-frame glasses made her already big blue eyes look giant.

She looked at the old man over the rims of her glasses. "What have we here?"

"Virgil Smith, ma'am. At your service. What's a pretty gal like you doin' wasting away in this one-horse town?"

Three Js had never seen Mrs. O'Leary blush in all the years he'd known her.

"Oh we got more'n a few horses in this town, Mr. Smith."

The old man grinned. "I bet you do. But I bet there aren't any other ladies as pretty as the one in here."

A smile Three Js didn't recognize on her face. "Deputy, what are we charging this silver-tongued devil with?"

"Murder, Mrs. O'Leary."

She nodded. "Figures. Only admirer I've had in a decade and he's a killer."

The old man scoffed. "Don't you believe it, Mrs. O'Leary. Just a large type misunderstanding."

She rolled her eyes, but the smile stayed put.

"Tell me, Mrs. O'Leary, does Mr. O'Leary know how lucky he is?"

"I reckon he did." She was getting paperwork ready for the prisoner. "Before he got himself shot."

"Was he a lawman?"

She nodded. "A federal marshal."

"Well I'm mostly sorry to hear that."

"Only mostly?"

He winked at her. "Only mostly."

Again, a bloom of pink on her cheeks.

"Dios mio, Mrs. O. This man shot old Sal three times in cold blood. Mr. Smith, kindly shut up while we fingerprint you."

"Can I help you there, Deputy?"

Three Js sighed. He handed her the prisoner's license. "Here, enter that into the system, please."

She frowned. "Yessir."

Once the prisoner was properly booked, Three Js locked him in one of the two adjoining cells then removed the handcuffs. "Make yourself comfortable."

The old man looked almost grateful at the familiar sight of iron bars.

"I suppose you'll be needing a lawyer?"

"I suppose I will. Know anybody?"

"I'm surprised he isn't here yet."

* * *

Dave Barry looked impressive in his neatly pressed khaki suit, perfectly knotted blue silk tie and shiny brown cowboy boots. He pulled a chair in front of Teddy's cell and sat. A yellow legal pad in his lap. A Mont Blanc pen in his hand. He observed Teddy for a minute. Another goddamn lawyer, Teddy thought, as he sipped the coffee the attorney had brought him.

"Did you do it?"

Teddy chuckled. "You start with all your clients like this?"

"Not all of them. Most of the ones charged with murder."

"Get a lot of killers in these parts?"

"This is the wild west, Mr. Smith. And you still haven't answered my question."

It occurred to Teddy that he could make a nice deal here. Give Palermo up in exchange for immunity. Maybe get relocated himself. A new life, a new name, a clean slate. Just like Sally. Wouldn't that be ironic.

"Did you know the deceased?"

Teddy is careful not to allow himself to grin. To give in to the warmth his heart feels at the memory of finally killing Sally C.

"Sally. The man who was killed."

An event he'd imagined for decades, so often it almost seemed like it couldn't have actually happened, like finally bedding a woman you'd dreamed of for years.

He'd never liked Sally. Never trusted him. With Wicked Bill in the hospital, Palermo had needed some extra muscle, an enforcer. But collecting debts is not all about breaking limbs. It's about the threat of broken limbs. Or worse. This was Wicked Bill's great gift. He knew how to make people fear him. The horror scene Teddy had witnessed was simply another tale of Bill's legendary cruelty.

Sally C was just another bully. He liked to shove people around. Liked to slap them. People didn't fear Sally, they hated him. So they turned on him. An old man in Little Havana who owned a cigar shop even agreed to wear a wire. That son of a bitch. Once Sally was arrested, he gave up every-body he could.

Yes, Teddy could cut a deal. But he wouldn't. He just wasn't built that way.

"No. I never saw an old man at the diner. Don't know him. Didn't kill him."

The lawyer nodded. Scribbled something in his legal pad. Sipped his coffee. "So that's our story?"

Our story. "That's my story."

"And you're sticking to it?"

"That's right."

"Fine by me. Now tell me the rest of your story. Start with what the hell you were doing driving down that particular road on this particular day."

Teddy had a rough sketch of a story prepared.

Given to him by his local contact, Ryan Murphy. He was here to do some hiking and got turned around. It's not like there were a lot of goddamned road signs in this part of the world.

The lawyer took notes and somehow kept from rolling his eyes.

"Then I drove away."

"A few miles later, you got a flat tire."

"These fucking roads out here."

"Maybe we have a case against the DOT."

"So what do you think?"

"I think if you're able to stick to that story, I might be able to keep you from the gas chamber."

"You might be able to?"

"Maybe. Depends how strong Doris' testimony is."

"Doris?"

"The waitress."

Dave Barry flipped his pad closed and put it in his satchel.

"So what's the next step?"

"Monday, we go before Judge Kelly for a bail hearing. Bail will be refused."

"Okay."

"Okay." Dave stepped close to the bars. "You think about that bullshit story of yours. You know the witness, or someone put you up to this, maybe I've got something I can sell to the judge. Stick to that story, it's your word against the waitress' and maybe the cook's." He put his Stetson on. "I'll be in touch."

Teddy watched him go. The feeling of deja vu hadn't left him since he'd been placed in the back of the police car.

16

Wicked Bill landed at the Tucson International Airport, a few asphalt runways in the middle of a vast, brown land rimmed by mountains and blue sky. He couldn't help thinking he'd arrived nowhere.

It was hot. He'd expected hot. Was used to it.

He rented a Chevy pickup at Budget with a fake Arizona driver's license. From there he drove to a sporting goods shop on the outskirts of the city called Desert Sports & Outdoors. He found all he needed to pose as a hiker: shorts, boots, tent, backpack. Then he strolled into the firearms section. He'd meant to buy a simple Glock 9 mm but he fell in love with a Beretta 92A1. He bought that and let himself be talked into a Windham SRC .308 rifle.

"You fixin' to do some hunting, partner?"

"I am."

"Well these'll put down whatever you're after."

"I think you're right."

Arizona was a nice state to purchase weapons in. No waiting period. All you needed was a license and a clean record.

According to the GPS on his phone, Bill was two hundred forty miles away from Yuma. He looked at the map on the screen which he knew wasn't doing justice to the hellish drive west through not much of anything. He sighed and put the truck in gear.

He eyed the vast horizon and thought of ancient times, when people thought the world just ended, like a cliff that you could fall off. Soon there was nothing but road, a Mad Max, post-apocalyptic landscape. He wasn't prepared for it. All that sky, all this sand. Overwhelming. Dizzying. He looked at the map for comfort, for reassurance that there was something where he was headed.

It occurred to him that he would have to make the same journey back. He already dreaded it.

He missed Miami. That blue blue ocean, the white sand. Not this brown dirt. Christ. These rocks. He craved the lush green, the palm trees, even the rain. South Beach. Ocean Boulevard. The pink-and-yellow art deco hotels, the clubs, the women. What he wouldn't give for a Cuban from Versailles right now.

No. He had a job to do. A mess to clean up. Ryan Murphy had let him down. He didn't care about the details of why. Until everyone was eliminated, they were exposed.

He stretched his neck left until it popped, then right. Better. Time to focus. Teddy was in custody. And two witnesses.

Needed to get the lay of the land. Scout the local

PD. But he decided to stop and eat and spend the night on the outskirts of Tucson. Enjoy what passed for civilization out here for another few hours. Maybe Ryan Murphy would surprise him, take care of what needed taking care of. Bill doubted it.

He'd head out in the morning. Fresh and rested. A hiker eager to hit the trail.

17

Cass drove Jeremiah's old pickup home. She headed west toward a low, orange sun. Her cheeks were flushed, probably from the heat, but maybe the day's activity as well. She'd done well. Shooting and helping with the fence. A full day. Now her eyes were droopy. So were his, to tell the truth.

"You tired?"

"I'm okay." She readjusted her grip on the wheel. Opened her eyes wider.

"Want me to drive?"

"Nope. Take a nap, Papa."

"Okay."

He chuckled, lowered his hat over his face. She knew the way. It wasn't far. He tried to picture the future for her. Would she stay? Find a man, settle down. Hard to picture. But he tried. Tried to see her with kids of her own. Imagined her, maybe with her own fierce daughter. Would she teach her daughter any of the things he'd taught her?

A scene came to him. Cass, a full-grown woman, bent on one knee, teaching her daughter how to aim. How to hold a pistol. The daughter asks who taught her that. My Papa, Cass says.

That's all the legacy Jeremiah needed. That moment would please him, even if he went to Hell. Christ he was getting sentimental in his old age. Something about this girl.

"Sing me a song, Papa."

"What kind of song?" he always asked. But it was always the same song. The song he sang to his sons, in happy times, before their mother passed.

"The cowboy song."

He sighed in mock annoyance, cleared his throat. "You asked for it, kid. My home's in Montana," he bellowed, "I wear a bandanna." She joined him now. "My spurs are of silver, my pony is gray."

The truck crested a hill and the ranch house was in sight. A black Jeep Wrangler was in the driveway. Jeremiah stopped singing. He knew that vehicle.

"Why'd you stop, Papa?"

Then she looked where he was looking.

"Who's that?"

"Unless I'm mistaken, that's your Uncle Ryan."

Her face lit up and Jeremiah tried very hard to keep his expression neutral.

"Do you think he brought me a present?"

"Let's go find out."

She squirmed in her seat as they approached. Jeremiah attempted to identify the swirl of emotions inside him. A churning cocktail that tasted most strongly of regret, with hints of anger and resentment. What had his boy done now? Jeremiah couldn't help but wonder. And mixed with the bitter feelings, he could detect a few faint traces of pride as well as the unpleasant, unfamiliar whiff of envy at Cass' reaction to her uncle.

She was out the door as soon as she put the truck in park, sprinting to Ryan who looked thin and tired and in need of a shave. He greeted the girl with open arms and lifted her off the ground in a twirl. She giggled.

Jeremiah scowled.

"Did you bring me anything?"

Ryan held his hands out, empty, like a magician. Then he snatched behind her ear and produced a bracelet.

"Would I ever come empty-handed?"

Another hug.

Jeremiah spit.

"Where's your daddy?"

"Out chasing bad guys, I'm told."

"Fighting the good fight, no doubt. How you doing, Jeremiah?" he asked without looking at his father.

"Fair to middlin'."

"Been a while, hasn't it?"

"A good bit of water under the bridge." Jeremiah remembered the last time he'd seen his oldest son.

18

Ryan didn't like to sleep, afraid of the memories that waited for him, dreams of war—the bombs, the blood, the dead friends, the slaughtered enemies. He preferred the utter emptiness of blackouts, the soothing numbness only buckets of booze could provide.

Six months he'd been out and hadn't done much sober in that time.

Get help, people told him. Some therapy, some drugs. But he couldn't. The part of him that asked for help had been broken somewhere along the way. Maybe on that fateful night with Leo in their yard. He was the one who helped.

It was the same in Iraq. Not a mark on him. His brothers in arms would call for him, wounded in the desert night, and he would find them, just like he found Leo in the blind vastness. But he couldn't rescue all of them.

He held their hands as their death grips grew limp, spoke to them until they couldn't speak back.

The iron scent of blood in his nose, its taste in his mouth.

Ryan came to in the Quicksilver drunk tank. Not a clue how he'd arrived there.

A whispered conversation in Spanish roused him. He thought he heard the word "Oscuro," but they might have just been describing their surroundings.

Besides Ryan and the two Mexicans, there were eight other men, all sleeping it off. The smells of bodily functions were overwhelming. Piss, sweat, shit, vomit, a combination that made it hard to breathe. The toilet was a toxic cauldron of vileness and appeared to have backed up, unwilling to consume any more filth.

The Mexicans whispered about someone called "El Jefe."

A fat man in the corner groaned in his sleep.

Another man in a tuxedo cradled his head and wept quietly to himself.

From far down the hallway outside the cell, footsteps and a high-pitched whistling came closer. It took Ryan a moment to place the tune. "The World Owes Me a Livin'." The whistler came closer until he stood in front of the cell. He was older than the last time he'd seen him, balder, with a touch of gray in his short hair.

"Hello, Ryan."

"Hello, Glenn."

"Let's go."

The cell door slid open. Ryan didn't need to be

asked twice. The other guests of the state watched like dogs do when their owners eat a meal, quiet and ready and hungry. *What about me?* Then Glenn slammed the door shut.

"Hold tight, amigos. Try to sleep it off."

Glenn led Ryan down the hallway, up a flight of stairs, through a few locked doors, to a big room with a dozen cubicles. Glenn sat at a desk, motioned for Ryan to take a chair.

"What the fuck?"

Ryan looked at his boots. "Just blowing off some steam."

Glenn had the report in front of him. He bent to read it. "Perpetrator assaulted three patrons of The Wagon Wheel. Victims suffered one broken nose, broken ribs, multiple contusions." Glenn skimmed the rest to himself. "I heard you put Bobby in a choke hold. Thank Christ he didn't put it in the report."

Ryan cleared his throat. He was perspiring. "He dared me to do that."

"Another dare gone wrong?"

Ryan grimaced. Hung his head.

"Look, if you're mad at your daddy, go kick his ass. You gotta find an outlet for that aggression that doesn't involve beating up my citizens. Okay, asshole?"

"Okay."

"Look at me."

Ryan met eyes with him.

"How's your brother? How's his leg?"

"Okay. Still loses feeling from time to time."

"Tell him I said hey."

Glenn nodded.

"Stop making us stick our necks out for you."

"Alright."

"And tell your daddy he's an asshole."

"He knows."

"Good." Glenn handed him a thick manila envelope with his belongings.

Ryan poured the contents into his hand. A wallet and his dog tags. Ryan hadn't removed them since he came home.

"Get the hell out of here, soldier."

Ryan chuckled. "Not anymore." He rubbed the tags together. "You serve?"

"Marines. Seventy-two to seventy-seven. Saw more jungle than I cared for."

"Nam?"

He shook his head. "A little Cambodia. Lots of red scares to quiet down."

"So you know…"

Glenn sighed. "I know coming home is no picnic. But you gotta stop picking fights with the world."

"Thanks, Glenn." He held out his hand.

"You're welcome. Don't make me regret this."

According to the last census, the town of Viejas held fifty-eight residents. What that number doesn't explain is that when the census taker, a fellow by the name of Beckham, knocked on his last door, he was greeted by a double-barrel shotgun, an antique American Arms Silver 12 gauge, held by a cranky, gray-haired Vietnam vet, Johnny Mahew, who suggested that the census taker wrap up his census taking immediately. Beckham chose not to argue. So fifty-eight became the official population, a few hundred shy of reality, but the reality was that the citizens of Viejas had come to live off the grid.

Years ago, when cinnabar had been harvested by the truck full out of the ground, the population had risen to over a thousand. The ruins of the mine and the surrounding buildings turned into a ghost town and that's what it was called. Betty Edwards ran a gift shop there selling history books and native American trinkets, mostly Comanche arrowheads and jewelry.

Not far from the center of the ghost town, Johnny Mahew ran a bar called The Cave. Semi-famous, it had made *Men's Journal's* top ten list of American dives. Tuesday night was cowboy poetry night and you never knew who might show up. Once the Drive By Truckers' tour bus had broken down on their way to Phoenix. They came in for some food and wound up playing until three in the morning. Like a lot of things in this part of the world, it became the stuff of legend.

Mahew served cold beer and warm barbecue and the locals who frequented the establishment offered plenty of color. War veterans, outlaws on the lam, and rangers from the national park thirty miles north.

A trailer park had sprung up next to The Cave, known locally as Drunk Town. It wasn't uncommon to find bodies littering the ground outside The Cave in the morning, customers who couldn't quite make it home. Everybody figured it beat having a pack of drunks driving around the desert in the middle of the night.

Mahew got his power from a windmill and a few dozen solar panels. He let Drunk Town bum power from him. Water came from a well and a few massive cisterns. A satellite provided a television signal. There was one phone located behind the bar. Sometimes Mahew had to call Jeremiah Murphy to arrange for medical attention after a fight or a serious fall.

The Cave was a place that asked no questions other than what was your poison. The perfect joint for Ryan to do some heavy drinking and heavy thinking. Most folks knew who he was, who his father was. They let him be with his shots of Beam and Lone Star chasers.

Two familiar faces.

The Mexicans from the drunk tank.

They nodded at Ryan in recognition. He nodded back. When did they get here? Would have thought they'd be on a bus back over the border. Odd.

He ordered another round. On a whim, he ordered one for the Mexicans.

They raised their glasses. One's teeth were perfect, the other's wouldn't have looked out of place on a jack-o-lantern. Their cheers sounded like Speedy Gonzalez before taking off.

Then they were next to him, clinking glasses, slapping his back. More rounds. They laughed at his bad Spanish. They didn't know much more than curses in English. The tall one with the nice teeth was Pablo. The one with the scorpions tattooed on his hands was Manuel. Call him Manny, he said. Pablo shared his Camels with no filters.

Ryan asked what they were doing in jail.

They winked, they nudged. "Same as you, ese."

"Meeting con El Jefe."

Ryan nodded. Raised his glass. "El Jefe."

They parroted him. "El Jefe!"

Ryan didn't know what they were talking about. Chalked it up to being drunk.

Manny and Pablo whispered to each other, quick and quiet in Spanish Ryan couldn't follow.

He let their conversation drift to the background. Tried to remember what day it was. Didn't have a clue. Thinking about what day it was raised the question of what day tomorrow was and he definitely didn't want to think about tomorrow, or the day after that. The future was a subject he studiously avoided. Clearly he wasn't quite drunk enough. He ordered another round.

"Mira, amigo." Manny thrust a wrinkled piece of paper at him. "Conoces donde esta?"

Ryan downed his shot of Beam and looked at the scrawled writing on the paper in blue ink. An address. He did a double, then a triple take. Couldn't understand why his father's address, Ryan's old address, was written there. This was really wrecking his buzz. He was aware of them watching him. He smiled. "Claro que si." *Of course I know.*

They grinned their ugly grins.

"Vamonos. Let me show you."

Ryan paid the bill. The Mexicans cheered.

He had to fight the hazy drunk his brain had become, like a swarm of bees in his skull. He had a pistol in his glove compartment. How could he get it?

They stepped outside. He was shocked to see the sun hanging low in the horizon. Felt like midnight.

"I have a map in my car," he told them in Spanish.

Everything surreal. The sky lavender, the sun a liquid pink, neat rows of clouds. The surrounding land desolate, beautiful. He was tempted to ask them to see the address again, doubted his own eyes. How could it be his family's ranch?

He wanted another drink, another cigarette. Almost wished he was back in Iraq. This would make sense there. People got shot every day there. It was war. What was this? What was he doing? He leaned against his car, took a deep breath.

"Esta bien, amigo?" Pablo asked.

Ryan nodded. "Just un poco boracho."

He unlocked the car. Opened the passenger door. How did he know they were going to do something to his father? Maybe they were just dropping off a package. He looked at them. He knew. He reached into the glove box. The familiar handle, familiar weight. No time to check it. It was locked and loaded. He was sure. His guns were like well-tended plants. He cleaned and oiled them once a month without fail.

The gun in his hand calmed him. He pushed out a breath. He came out of the car, wobbly but his aim was true. He hit Pablo in the chest.

Manny's sleepy eyes came wide awake. "Que pasa?"

"Lo siento, amigo."

Another shot and Manny's eyes went to sleep for good.

Ryan fought the temptation to go back inside and get a drink, explain the situation. It did occur to him to find the piece of paper with his father's address on it. He took Pablo's cigarettes while he was at it.

From the bar he could hear Emmylou Harris. "Waltz Across Texas." One of his favorites. He got in his car. Turned the key. Stomped on the gas.

He drove fast along the lonely highways of Oscuro County. Night enveloped him. Horizons laden with stars in every direction. As a kid he would pretend he was an astronaut hurtling through space in the back of his daddy's pickup truck.

Found himself in Quicksilver. At the Dairy Queen. He stood in line with a bunch of kids, toddlers squirmed and teenagers flirted. Tried to remember the last time he'd been here. Had to be years. A decade maybe. Probably with Leo. It tasted like being twelve years old—like first kisses and home-run swings. It had been a while since anything had tasted sweet. He savored it. Figured it would be a long while before he had another one.

He turned his headlights off about a mile before he arrived.

The lamp outside the kitchen glowed pale yellow, the only source of light, other than stars and moon, in sight. Such a familiar scene. Even when his brother had been bitten by that rattler, that light had comforted him. It meant home was within reach.

He stayed in his car, in the driveway, just watching. He jumped in his skin when the passenger door opened and Jeremiah sat down.

Still in his sheriff's uniform, he lit a cigarette, offered one to Ryan who declined. Jeremiah produced a flask and took a pull. When he offered it, Ryan accepted. The reliable bite of Jim Beam. Ryan handed it back. His father took another swig and tucked it away.

"That was quite a mess you left for me, son."

"I didn't see any other way."

A noise in his father's throat. A chuckle? "Not that cleaning up your messes is anything new. Just thank Christ your little brother wasn't involved in this one."

That old saw. Still stung every time his father brought it up. He thinks of the piece of paper with his father's address on it. This address. Evidence.

Justification for his actions maybe. But something makes him withhold it. Pride? He wants the knowledge over his father. Doesn't want him to know he saved his life. Not yet anyway.

"Witnesses place you at the scene of the crime, associating with the victims. I guarantee ballistics is a match to your sidearm. Only thing missing is motive but I'm sure a good prosecutor could bring your history of bar brawls up in court. We call this open and shut. Do you need anything out of the house?"

"What?"

"Maybe some clothes. Just what you can carry."

Ryan looked at his father in confusion.

Jeremiah sighed. "You're going on a trip, son. Over the border. Or under it rather."

Ryan was stunned and fully sober now. He was a fugitive. He was going on the lam. What shocked him the most was that his father was helping him.

"Now or never, son."

He nodded, opened his door. "I'll pack a bag."

"We'll need some food and water."

We?

Ryan put some clothes together, changed into a good pair of hiking boots. He touched his purple heart but left it. He'd have to send a note to Leo. Choked up when it dawned on him he didn't know when he'd see his brother again, when he'd be able to explain what happened.

Jeremiah came into his room carrying a backpack loaded with supplies. "Ready?"

"Yup. You identify those Mexicans?"

Jeremiah shrugged. "Couple of illegals. No ID. Might be cartel connections. The law might be the least of your problems."

So why did Glenn turn them loose, Ryan wondered.

They drove separate cars. He followed his father to the old mine. Fifty years ago it had employed over a hundred men, almost half of them Mexicans. That was how Ryan's great grandfather had made his fortune and bought all this land.

His father pulled to a stop. Ryan pulled next to him. They both got out.

Dark now, the silhouettes of the old mining buildings stood black against the starry sky. But not as black as the mouth of the mine. Dug at the bottom of a rocky hill that resembled a sneering monster.

"Hope you're not afraid of the dark." Jeremiah chuckled as he checked the light on a large, black flashlight. "This should get you there."

"Where?"

"Mexico, jackass."

"What? The border must be three miles away."

"Give or take. Tunnel runs just under four."

"What tunnel?"

Jeremiah grabbed the backpack out of his pickup. "Back in the day, it occurred to my granddaddy that it would be cheaper to use undocumented Mexican labor."

"Especially if they got sick or injured."

"I don't see you applying for sainthood any time soon." He scowled at Ryan.

Ryan scowled back.

"So he built his own little pipeline under the border. Once the mine closed, he didn't have any need of it. I found it by accident as a kid. Exploring where I wasn't supposed to explore. We might be the only two people who know about it now."

Four miles. Underground. In the dark. Ryan hoped his father didn't notice him shiver at the thought.

"Where's it come out?"

"Wouldn't want to spoil the surprise. You'll be in San Polvo. There's a few other connections. One branch goes off into some Indian reservation territory. The Kumeyaay Tribe. Stay straight. You'll be okay. But until you get to the long straightaway you want to take every right turn at the fork."

Jeremiah handed him the backpack. Then he produced an envelope. "Some cash here. Just what I could scrape together."

Ryan didn't know what to say.

"Things'll cool off eventually. Lay low for now. There's a bar in the center of town. La Taza Vacía. Kid named Pedro works there. I can get word to you through him. And vice versa."

"Okay."

"I suppose there's a lot of bullshit we could say

to each other right now. A lot of thank yous and sorrys and if onlys. I don't really feel like it. Do you?"

"No."

"Good." Jeremiah handed him the flashlight. "Remember. Right turns until it straightens out. Then stay straight until you hit the end."

"Got it."

Jeremiah held out his hand. Ryan took it. Couldn't remember the last time he'd touched his father.

"Best get a move on."

He took slow and careful steps into the Stygian tunnel. The flashlight beam revealed jagged rock walls and a low ceiling. A hundred yards in, train tracks appeared, orange with rust. The air was cool and damp, a breeze blew from behind him, pushed him deeper into the shaft.

At the first fork he turned right, the tunnel suddenly aimed steeply down, headed straight to Hell. Another few hundred yards and the passage leveled off but narrowed until Ryan could almost touch both sides at once.

He stopped and took a sip of water, tried to squelch the wave of claustrophobia gripping him. Wondered if he'd made it half a mile yet. Three and a half to go. Keep it together. Deep breath. He proceeded.

Ryan was well-acquainted with the dark. But

this close, suffocating blackness was something new. Everything pressed in on him. His eyes started to play tricks on him. In the shadows made by the flashlight beam, he saw creatures scatter then disappear when he shined the light at them.

He lost track of time and distance.

Just turned right at each fork.

An irrational part of him wondered if he'd ever get to the end. Had he died and gone to Hell? Sweaty palms held the flashlight too tight. The beam as shaky as his hands.

The occasional scurry and squeal of rats. At least he hoped they were just rats. He prayed not to hear a snake's rattle. That thought combined with the pitch black behind him made him perspire. He had to stop. Get control of his breathing.

Get a hold of yourself, man.

Another sip of water. Tasted dusty. He aimed the flashlight and followed the beam down the tunnel that seemed to shrink, just a little, with each step.

As the alcohol left his bloodstream, he pondered the men he'd killed, Pablo and Manny. Why had they been turned loose? If his father could find out their cartel connections in a few hours, surely Glenn would have known. *Meeting con El Jefe,* they'd said. *Same as you.*

Glenn had pulled some strings to get him out.

"Goddammit!" His voice rebounded off the cave walls, sent the rats scrambling.

He had to go back.

19

2012

Doris and Leo sat in Leo's Explorer. Too hot to sit outside and she didn't want to go back inside the diner. As she told him the details of what happened, Becker and a few assistants loaded the body into the ambulance. She wouldn't look in their direction.

"Then you and the rest of the cavalry showed up." She offered a tired smile.

"And you never saw the guy before?"

She shook her head. "My impression was he'd never been out this way before."

"This way?"

"Out west. He was east coast. Seemed like a fish out of water."

Leo pictured the old man they'd picked up. Nodded in agreement.

"Sal knew." She looked at the kitchen. Like she'd heard something.

"Knew what?"

"He knew somebody would come. He told me once. A man will come someday. Let him do what he has to do."

"Sounds like he did."

"Why would he know that? Why would a person want to hurt Sal?"

Leo grimaced. "Maybe Old Sal was no boy scout."

"Seriously?"

"I'm not supposed to say anything, but since he's dead, I guess it couldn't hurt anything."

Her eyes were wide in anticipation. Christ she was cute.

"Sal was in witness protection. Used to be a mobster in Miami."

"No shit?"

"No shit. He turned state's evidence on half a dozen bad guys. Half a dozen bad guys with an axe to grind."

"You think the old guy's one of them?"

"I'd bet money on it."

"You think you know a person."

"People let you know the person they want you to know."

She squinted at him. "In your line of work, you must see the person they don't want you to know. All their dirty little secrets."

"Everybody's got secrets."

"Even you?"

"Even me."

She gave him a sly look.

"Let me take you home."

"I'd like to go home."

"You okay to drive?"

"I think so."

"I'll follow you."

"You offer that service to all victims?"

"No."

She lived at the western edge of town in a small cluster of homes. Beyond her house were acres of desert until you reached the Oscuro Mountains. A tiny adobe-roofed house with a dirt yard and a carport, it matched her neighbors' homes. Doris rented the house from Gladys Delgado, the old lady who lived next door. She taught second grade at the elementary school for forever. Retired a few years ago. Still volunteered there a couple of days a week. If she was home, Leo was sure Mrs. Delgado was watching Leo pull in front of Doris' yard, thrilled to have some gossip to share with the other old hens in town.

Leo met Doris at the front door.

"I've got some sweet tea in the fridge if you like."

Leo took his hat off as he stepped inside. "That sounds fine."

"I might go for something stronger."

"Can't blame you."

The house was neat and spare. Unpainted white walls. Black-and-white photographs of desert landscapes at night. Doris led him to a room with a brown leather couch and a wicker chair. She motioned to the couch. He sat.

"Let me get you that tea."

"Thanks."

More pictures in this room. Same theme. One of the horizon scarred by lightning strikes. One of a huge moon taking up half the picture. Then one that made him stand and take a closer look. A view from a highway. No stars in the sky but little halos of light hovered unnaturally.

"The Diablo Lights," she said when she came back in holding a glass of iced tea in one hand and what looked like a gin and tonic in the other. "I spent a week cruising the old Imperial Highway. Only saw them the one night."

Leo's ankle throbbed as the memories rushed back. "I saw them once."

"Lucky."

He chuckled. "It wasn't a lucky night. I got bit by a rattler. My brother was driving me to the hospital. I was delirious. But that's just what they looked like."

She handed him the iced tea.

"Thanks." He took a sip. Good and cold. "You take all of these?"

"Yup. My hobby."

"I like them."

"I think that's what keeps me here."

"What?"

She looked up. "The big sky here. All those stars. Sometimes I walk out into the desert at night until all I can see is stars, like they're surrounding me."

"Careful you don't get bit by something."

"That must have been scary. How old were you?"

"I was about eight. Wasn't as scary as what you saw today."

She gulped her gin and tonic. "Something like this happens, you ponder the fact you're not gonna live forever. You know?"

"I know."

"You start thinking that you shouldn't put off what you want." Her eyes were an invitation.

Leo put his glass down. Stepped toward her. "What do you want?"

"Same as you, Sheriff. Don't make me beg."

It occurred to him only after they were kissing how long it had been since he'd felt a woman's lips. Then he was in a storm of sensations: the sweet taste of juniper on her tongue, the lingering scent of Sally's Diner in her hair, the sight of her closed eyes pushed next to his face, the hungry noises she made in her throat.

She noticed his eyes were open and pulled back, breathing heavy. "What?"

"Just enjoying the view."

They got back to it with gusto. Their hands started to roam. The notion that this was not the best idea, not the right time, flickered in his mind but he quickly snuffed it out. Decided thinking right now was a mistake.

She pulled away. "I'm gonna go freshen up.

Reckon I'll meet you in the back bedroom."

He watched her stand. As she walked out of the room she pulled off her shirt and dropped it on the floor. Leo didn't realize for a moment that his mouth hung wide open.

He pulled his boots and socks off then stood. His trick leg behaved itself as he stepped down the hallway. Running water from behind the closed bathroom door.

"Make yourself at home, Sheriff."

He unbuttoned his shirt, hung it on a chair. Took his pants off. Stood there in boxers and a tank top, wondered if he should keep going when he heard the bathroom door open. A childish part of him was nervous to turn around. If this were a dream, that's when it would end, denying him a look at her. The open door invited a breeze and he caught the sweet scent of her perfume.

He turned around.

Framed in the doorway in nothing but her panties, he drank in the sight of her. Broad shoulders, slender arms, his eyes drifted to her teardrop-shaped breasts, the widening flare of her hips.

"Come here," he said.

"Say please."

"Pretty please."

She swayed toward him, grinning, walking on the balls of her feet, catlike. When she reached him, she peeled off his shirt, moved her palms to his shoulders, to his chest, down his torso.

He pulled her to him, loving the firm feel of her skin against his. They stood in each other's arms, as though about to dance a tango. She kissed him, breathing hard out of her nose, pushing hard, he could feel her teeth against his. She leaned back, then they both fell onto her bed, giggling.

Their hands busy, priming each other.

"Let's just do it. Okay?"

"Okay."

Naked now. She lay on her back, hands on his shoulders. He pointed himself at her.

"Okay?"

"Yes yes yes yes."

He grinned and pushed and she surrounded him. He plunged deep. Deeper.

She gasped. Hands on his ass, pulling him. She groaned.

His grin bigger now.

Her mouth on his shoulder, biting.

He let a rhythm build, slowly. In and out. Their eyes met. All smiles.

She nodded. "Yes." Her eyes fluttered up, only the whites visible.

His pace quickened.

"Yes."

The scent of it all encompassing, everything moist. Fast now, and hard, now faster, harder.

She bit a pillow to quiet herself.

He took it away.

"There," she said. "Right there. Just like that."

He felt it build, his voice rose.

She nodded, she squeezed his arms, she hollered.

He let it come, his heart ready to explode.

She shrieked in release, wrapped her arms around him and embraced the air out of him. After she caught her breath, she said, "You okay?"

"Goddamn." He bit her neck.

"Want to do it again?"

Before he could answer, his phone buzzed.

"Goddamn."

A picture of Three Js on the display. He gave her an apologetic shrug.

"It's okay," she said.

He picked up his phone. "What's up, amigo?"

"So sorry to interrupt your interview, Sheriff."

"I bet you are."

"You know some women who survive deadly situations find it stimulating."

"That information better not be the only reason you called."

"Thought you should know. Just got a call from south of the border. They found somebody we're looking for."

"Angel?"

Her eyes went big.

"Sí, señor. But he ain't in any shape to question, if you catch my drift."

"I catch it." He let out a long sigh. "Shit. How'd it go down?"

"Few miles out of Pachuco. Looks like Angel

was making a run for it. Somebody didn't let that happen."

"Where was it?"

"On Highway Two. Middle of nowhere. No witnesses. I might go take a look. I know the federales investigating."

"I'll meet you."

"You sure you don't got better things to do?"

"And when I meet you, I'm gonna smack that shit-eating grin off your face."

Three Js' deep laugh answered him. "Ten four, sheriff."

Leo ended the call, looked at Doris. "Shit."

"He's dead?" Sad eyes, maybe a little scared.

"Yup."

"What happened?"

"I'm gonna go find out."

"Never figured you for the love 'em and leave 'em type."

"I'm sorry."

"I'm kidding. Go find out what happened."

He started to dress.

She went into the bathroom, came out in a white terry-cloth robe.

His head spun from the events of the day. Two murders now, some long overdue amorous activity. A lot to process.

She walked out of the bedroom to the front of the house.

"Do you have someone you can stay with?" he

called to her.

He heard her rummaging in a closet.

"Don't you worry about me, Sheriff."

He pulled on his pants and walked to the living room. Doris was loading a shotgun.

"I can take care of myself." Her face was fierce as she snapped the rifle closed and placed it on the coffee table. Took a sip from her gin and tonic.

It was one of the sexier sights he'd ever seen.

"Don't get too deep into that gin."

"Just enough to calm my nerves. It improves my aim."

"I have to go."

"I know."

"I don't want to."

"I don't want you to either."

"When all this is over…"

"Come by any time, Sheriff."

"You're a hell of a pretty girl, Doris."

"You're no slouch yourself, Leo."

"I think that's the first time you ever used my name."

"I reckon we should be on a first-name basis now."

"I reckon."

She stepped close and tilted her face up to his. A quick kiss turned into a slow one.

He went out the door savoring the taste of her on his lips.

20

"Lousy place to get shot," Three Js said.

It was.

A desolate stretch of Carretera Federal 2. The road had been bleached by the sun until it was the color of the sand surrounding it. Angel's pickup looked out of place here. It belonged in Sally's parking lot back in Oscuro. The only place Leo had ever seen it. Now photos were being snapped of the poor kid's corpse.

A federale Leo knew a bit walked over.

"Hell of a day, Sheriff."

"That's for sure."

His English was excellent. Leo wondered how he kept from perspiring in his uniform in this heat.

"We get a time of death?"

"Not long. Couple hours."

"Cause?"

"Gunshot to the head. Messy."

The second one, today, Leo thought. He walked over to the vehicle. He leaned in for a glimpse. Angel's eyes were still open. The back of his head was littered all over the upholstery. "Who did you see, amigo?"

Three Js approached. "Spoke to my friend."

"And?"

"From the tire tracks, looks like another vehicle forced Angel off the road. Bang bang."

Leo spit. "What the fuck? So another pro?"

"Somebody covering tracks."

"What was the murder weapon?"

"Nine millimeter. Nothing exotic."

Leo couldn't help but picture his brother. Ryan in his black Jeep coming up fast behind Angel's ancient pickup. Forcing him off the road. Too easy. Fast and efficient. The way the army trained him.

But why? Who was he protecting?

"I need to talk to the old man," Leo said.

"This seems like a lot of trouble to go to."

"Must be something big behind it."

"You think the old man will give it up?"

"Only one way to find out."

Three Js came close to Leo, grinning. He took a whiff. "How'd things go with Doris?"

"I warned you about that grin, Deputy."

The grin got bigger. "Perdon, Señor. Hey, I think it's a good thing, hombre. Long overdue."

"Anyway, I'll meet you at the station. I gotta check on the kid. Hang out in case there's any surprises here."

"Will do."

Leo pause before getting in his car. Looked at

155

Three Js. "So if somebody's cleaning things up, there's two more loose ends to tie up."

Three Js held up two fingers. "Doris." He thought. "What's the second?"

"The old man."

A slow nod from Three Js. "If they're really serious."

Leo looked at Angel's lifeless corpse. "They look pretty serious to me."

"Maybe I go right to the station."

"See you there."

Another thought occurred to Leo. "Deputy?"

"Yes, Sheriff?"

"If Angel has no papers, what happens to him?"

Three Js chewed his lip. "I'll see if I can't locate his family. At least he's on this side of the border."

"You're a good hombre, hombre."

Three Js waved as he headed to his cruiser.

21

Leo chewed events over in his head as he drove. He tried to focus on what couldn't be seen. Somebody put the old man onto Sal. Ryan wouldn't do it for free. There's somebody between Ryan and the old man. Somebody with money. His eyes drifted to the horizon, as though he might find Ryan there. As if Ryan would let himself be found.

When he came over the last rise and saw the ranch a surprise lay in wait. His brother's jeep next to the house. He searched his mind to think of some other explanation. Could it be someone else in the same make and model and color of car? Not likely. Years of police work teach you it's usually the simplest answer.

He pulled next to it. Stepped out of his vehicle. His eyes were so drawn to it he barely registered his daughter rushing out of the house to see him.

"Daddy, it's Uncle Ryan."

"How about that."

"He said later he'd take me for a ride in his jeep."

"Did he now?"

"He did. You don't seem so excited."

"Oh I'm excited. Where is my big brother?"

"In the back. Up on the ridge."

Leo saw him now. In the perfect place to spot someone coming. Ryan was always watching his back.

"Where's Papa?"

"In the kitchen. Making dinner I think."

"Go help him, would you?"

"But I want to go see Uncle Ryan."

"Later, kid. Let me and him catch up in private."

She pouted. Opened her mouth to protest.

"I said later."

She stormed inside.

He walked toward his brother's lean silhouette. Ryan turned in a slow circle, surveyed the horizon in every direction. Satisfied, he moved toward Leo. Before long, Leo could see how thin his brother was, how tired his eyes were. The smile on Ryan's face looked forced. He needed a shower and a shave and a good meal.

"Hey, little brother."

"Hey, Ryan."

"Cass got tall. What happened to that little girl I used to know?"

"Same thing that happened to us. She got older."

Ryan slipped a silver flask out of his back pocket and unscrewed it. Leo caught the scent of Bushmills in the air. Ryan took a healthy pull. Offered it to Leo who took it. He welcomed the sting in his throat, then handed it back.

"What a bleak goddamned place."

"It's home."

"Home." Ryan slipped the flask in his pocket.

Leo held up two fingers. "Two murders today, big brother. I figure you pulled the trigger on the second. Reckon you pointed the killer in the direction of the first. Tell me I'm wrong."

Ryan looked down at his boots, let out a sigh, like somebody had poked a hole in him. If Leo didn't know him better, he'd almost say he looked sorry.

But not Ryan.

"Little brother, we got much bigger problems than those two murders."

"We?"

Ryan winced. Nodded.

"We, like you and me? Or we, like you, me, Dad, and Cass?"

"It was such a sweet fucking plan, man. Nobody got hurt except some goddamned outlaws that had it coming anyway."

"Then the old man got a flat tire."

"Then the old man got a fucking flat tire."

"Who is he?"

"Old button man, name of Teddy McCarthy."

"One of the guys Sally put away?"

"Yup. Dude did twenty years."

"So now what?"

"The boss I set this up with in Miami wants

things cleaned up."

"Like you cleaned things up with Angel?"

"There's a guy on his way into town. Goes by the handle Wicked Bill. They don't call him that because he's a fan of the Wizard of Oz. This is a guy you don't want to meet."

"What are you saying?"

"I'm saying there's two ways to handle this. The easy way or the hard way."

"What's the easy way?"

"Kill the old man and the waitress."

Leo's heart clenched at the mention of Doris. A flurry of images of her in his brain.

"What's the hard way?"

"Don't."

Leo felt every muscle in his body tense, his neck quivered, his hands shook. "Guess which way we're going to do it?" He was prepared to kill his brother just then.

"Little brother, I need you to think."

Leo swung his right fist as hard as he could at his brother's head. But Ryan saw it coming yesterday and just batted it away.

"You're a smart guy, Leo. Think of what your family is worth to you."

Now he came with the left, then a combination. Ryan was ahead of every punch. Worse, he didn't hit back. Just dodged the blows.

"Aren't they worth an old criminal and some white trash waitress?"

Leo lowered his shoulder and heard a horrible noise escape his mouth as he crashed into Ryan. The two of them went down but Ryan used Leo's momentum to spin him in the air and he landed hard on his back. Ryan sprang to his feet. Leo got up much slower.

"Daddy, what are you doing?"

Jeremiah was holding her back. "Let them settle it themselves, sweetheart."

Ryan was grinning. "So that's it? The waitress?" He rolled his eyes.

Leo rushed him again.

"Easy, lawman." Ryan's leg was a blur as it extended and his right foot connected with Leo's solar plexus, knocking the wind out of him.

"Daddy!" She pulled away from Jeremiah, rushed up the ridge.

"Okay okay okay!" Ryan held his hands up. "We do it the hard way, asshole. For your girl."

Leo was on all fours, trying to suck in air.

Cass touched his shoulder. "You okay, Daddy?"

Shame flooded his bloodstream, painted his face red. Compounded by the fact Leo couldn't speak, couldn't seem to make the air cooperate with his lungs.

"He's just got to catch his breath, Cass."

"Why'd you kick him, Uncle Ryan?"

"Because he's a jackass, Cass. Just like your father." Jeremiah looked highly amused.

Ryan looked at him like he didn't recognize him.

Because with the smile on his face, he didn't.

"Just like your grandfather for that matter."

"Took the words right out of my mouth, Pops," Ryan said.

"Okay, dummies. Dinner is served. Let's go."

Leo stood, still woozy.

Cass shot him a concerned look.

"I'm okay, kid. Let's eat."

22

Love or money, Ryan thought as he walked back to the house. The two elemental motives. He'd always thought love was for suckers. Always let dollar signs point him in the right direction. Almost always. And on those rare occasions when his heart led him, hadn't it always been a mistake? The shootout at The Cave, protecting his father. Hadn't been a dime in that. Now he was a fugitive, a man without a country.

Then there was Leo.

Everything he did, he did for love.

Even when he took Ryan's dirty payoffs, he was looking after his daughter, providing for her.

But look what love had done to him. Or their father for that matter. Both of their marriages had ruined them. Better not to get attached, Ryan had learned. Live like a rolling stone.

Once inside, Ryan was thrown by the familiar scent of his father's spaghetti and meatballs. As children this had been their Sunday night meal. The one recipe of their mother's that Jeremiah could recreate.

The meal had made him think of his mother then and it made him think of her now. In his childhood home the memories came easier. Her voice calling him for supper, or singing a lullaby at bedtime. She was a country music fan, always humming something by Patsy Cline or Loretta Lynn.

"Smells good, Papa," Cass said and bolted to the dining room table. "Uncle Ryan, you sit here, next to me."

They all took their old places at the table, Cass in their mother's chair. An unwelcome sensation of nostalgia in Ryan's gut. He wanted to get the hell out of here.

Cass was full of questions. She hadn't seen her uncle in years.

"So you grew up here?"

"Yup."

"Where did you sleep?"

"End of the hall."

"That's where my daddy slept."

"We shared a room."

The food was simple, but good. Stirred up more memories. His mother asking him about school, about his teacher, Mrs. Castle. Ryan didn't like her. She was mean. Why? She made him do math worksheets. He remembered resenting his mother's laughter at the time but now, the ghostly echo of it in his head was warm and welcome.

"Did you guys fight when you were little too?"

"Like cats and dogs," Jeremiah said.

"That's what brothers do," Leo said.

"My job was to toughen Leo up. That's what big brothers do."

A skeptical look on Cass' face as she stuffed a forkful of pasta in her mouth. She chewed as she spoke. "But you saved him when he got bit by the snake."

Ryan noticed Jeremiah's jaw clench at the reference, same as his. All three men tensed at their own private memories of that night.

"Who told you that?"

"Daddy. And Papa."

"Well I drove him to the hospital."

"How old were you?"

"About as old as you are now."

She thought about that. Chewed her food. Swallowed. "That's pretty brave."

"You would have done the same thing."

She frowned. "I don't think most people would have."

"I didn't say most people. I said you."

"Why did you kick Daddy?"

"I thought it might make him listen to reason."

"It is tough to get him to do that."

"He's stubborn. Always was."

Ryan couldn't understand how Leo could risk harm coming to a hair on this child's head. This waitress must be some piece of ass.

"Where do you live now?"

"Oh, around. Mostly down south."

"In Mexico?"

"Sí señorita."

"Do you like it?"

"I never really thought about it." He noticed Leo and Jeremiah were as interested in his answers as Cass. "Do you like living here?"

"It's okay. But I've never lived anywhere else so I can't compare it to anything. You've been all over, haven't you?"

"All over."

"What's your favorite place?"

Funny. His eyes rarely went to the good in a place. He recounted the squalor he'd seen wherever he went. The innocent victims of IEDs in Iraq and Afghanistan. The wounded, the dead, the blood, and the suffering war left in its wake. He'd been to Berlin for R&R but he only saw it at night, red neon and women in bar light. He slept all day. Never saw the sights.

Fort Bragg was a blur of running and shooting and drills and wargames.

There was really only one place he had fond memories of. It happened to be the place he had the worst memories from.

His favorite place was right here.

Ain't that a bitch.

"I'll have to think about it, Cass. I've been a lot of places."

"Have you been to Hawaii?"

"Nope."

"I think that would be my favorite place."

"Make your dad take you to see the ocean some time."

"You hear that, Daddy?"

"I hear it."

"Will you take me?"

"Yes."

"Promise?"

"I promise."

When they were finished, Jeremiah and Cass cleared the table and did the dishes. Leo called the station to check in. Ryan took the half full beer he had left and walked outside.

The stars were just puncturing a sky the color of a bruise, dark blue, light black. He heard his mother again. That group there is the Pleiades. Then she would tell him the Greek myth it came from. There's your sign, the hunter. And your brother's, the lion. At night, when Ryan looked at the sky, he saw Greek heroes and villains and heard his mother's voice.

He should never have come back here.

All these phantom memories were making it hard to concentrate, making him lose his edge.

Here was Leo coming up next to him. He waited for a minute before he spoke. They were probably a few feet from where the rattler had taken a bite out of him. Maybe not even.

"Can you watch Cass for me tonight?"

"Where will you be?"

"Guarding Teddy McCarthy."

"Need help?"

"I don't think I'm gonna let you within ten feet of that old man."

"Why not ask Dad?"

"This guy you're talking about shows up, dad won't be able to hold him off."

"You think I can?"

"I do, big brother."

"What about your girl?"

"Unless you give him the intel, he'll have to do a little digging to find her."

"Just think about giving them up, man. Everybody would be safe. No looking over your shoulder."

"I'm tired of looking the other way."

"You want to be the knight in shining armor."

"I just want to be the good guy. I don't want any more blood on my conscience unless they deserve it."

"So you'll protect a guy like Teddy McCarthy?"

"I'll keep him in jail. Will you watch Cass?"

"Yes."

"Three Js will trade with me at dawn. I'll be back then."

"Nothing will happen to her."

"Promise?"

"I promise."

23

The center of town was church quiet. The only lights on came from the police station and Leo's headlights. He parked next to Three Js' cruiser, rolled up his windows, and stepped out.

Three Js was at his desk, reading the paper. "Evening, Sheriff."

"Evening, Deputy. How goes it?"

"Fine. Virgil here's a model prisoner."

"He have anything valuable to say?"

"Nope. He's made quite an impression on Mrs. O'Leary though."

"Come again?"

"The old lady is warm for his form, as the kids like to say."

"Mrs. O?"

"Virgil had her blushing and everything."

Leo was dumbfounded. "It's always these quiet, church-going gals you have to keep an eye on."

Three Js shrugged. "Only the good die young."

"Well, I got it from here, man. Head home."

Three Js stood. "I'll see you when the cock crows."

Leo watched him get in his car and leave. Then he locked and bolted the front door.

He'd been tempted to tell Three Js the truth about Teddy McCarthy, but he didn't want to endanger him if he didn't have to. And he didn't want to get into the details of his relationship with Ryan or the particulars of Angel's death. He didn't think Three Js would be able to let that slide.

He walked back toward the cells. There had been no movement while they'd talked. As he got closer, he saw Teddy's form on the cot to the left of the cell. He pulled a chair over, turned it backward, and sat with his arms folded on the back.

"You asleep, Teddy?"

The prisoner stirred.

Teddy cleared his throat. "What'd you call me?"

"I called you Teddy. Would you prefer Theodore? Or Mr. McCarthy?"

Teddy stretched, put his arms under his head. "My mother used to call me Theodore when I was in trouble. Sounds like somebody's been naming names. I'm gonna guess it's somebody with the same last name as you, Sheriff Murphy."

Leo smiled. "Since we're naming names."

"If you're here to kill me, Sheriff, I wish you'd just get to it." Teddy propped himself up on his elbows, looked at Leo with his hundred-yard gaze. "You'll find it's easier to do it quick when you're bumping somebody off."

"That's what you've learned?"

170

"In the school of hard knocks."

"I'm not here to kill you."

"Why are you here?"

"To keep somebody else from killing you."

Teddy raised his eyebrows. "Somebody like your brother?"

"Among others."

Teddy sat straight up now. "I can think of a few people who'd breathe easier if I was taking a dirt nap."

"What can you tell me about Bill?"

Leo saw a change in Teddy's face. Anger or fear, maybe both, caused his jaw to stiffen and his eyes to narrow. "I can tell you he's somebody you never want to meet."

"Something tells me I'm not going to be that lucky."

Teddy sighed. "He's about as bad as they come, Sheriff. And I've met my fair share of bad. He's not just in it for the money."

"What do you mean?"

"He enjoys it. Hurting people. Killing people. He gets off on it. And if you get on his bad side." Teddy shook his head. "God help you."

"Are you on his bad side?"

"Sure looks that way."

"What's he look like?"

"Ugly. Ugly inside and out."

"That's not so helpful."

"Burns. His face is covered in burn scars."

Leo squeezed his temples with his left hand. Bill sounded like a villain straight out of central casting. He couldn't help picturing Jack Palance from *Shane* with burns on his face. The events of the day had the unreal feel of an old Western.

"You might consider just getting out of his way."

"Let him kill you? And the girl at the diner?"

Teddy shrugged. "Bravery gets plenty of people killed."

"They already got the cook."

"That Mexican kid?"

"His name was Angel."

Teddy didn't care, didn't want to know his name. "For what it's worth, Sheriff, none of this was supposed to go down this way. A simple hit then run across the border."

Leo rubbed a hand down his face. "It's not worth too much now, is it?"

"I suppose not."

24

Ryan heard her stir, get out of bed.

He was out on the front porch. The stars were uncut diamonds on black felt. He listened to the wind, his ears strained for something out of place. A footstep, a cough, a breath. His eyes scanned the horizon for movement.

Nothing, until he caught the sound of Cass pushing her sheets off and getting out of bed.

He wondered what she would do. Did she need to use the bathroom? Would she call out?

He waited, swaying gently forward and back in his father's rickety old rocking chair, in the dark. The porch light would have messed with his night vision.

Cass' footsteps crept. Out of her room. Down the hall. She didn't call out. She was very quiet. He was impressed. He remembered sneaking in and out of the house as a teenager. He'd learned through practice the quiet places to step. Just like her.

There was a light on in the kitchen, same as when he was a kid. He watched her silhouette move into the room. Quiet and careful as a thief.

He grinned. Would she look outside now?

Part of him still listened for foreign sounds. The breeze picked up, the old windmill turned faster.

The screen door to the porch creaked open. He could sense her wincing at the noise. His sneaky niece.

She looked in his direction, her eyes still adjusting to the dark, he was just a shape—more shadow than flesh.

A low whisper. "Uncle Ryan?"

"Hi, Cass. Can't sleep?"

"No."

"What's wrong?"

"I had a bad dream."

"I remember when my mom was in the hospital giving birth to your dad I had terrible dreams. I thought that snakes were on the ceiling. Every night until she came back. What was yours about?"

"My mother."

"I have that dream all the time."

"About my mother?"

"About mine. Your grandmother."

"Daddy's mom?"

"Yup."

"I never knew her."

"Your father barely did. She died too young."

"Were you sad?"

"Very sad."

"My mommy left us too."

"I know, kid."

"We don't know where she went. Or where she is."

"Come here." He put his pistol on a table next to the chair and held open his arms.

She sat on his lap. The tears came now. He rubbed her back for a long while.

Later he said, "After my mom was gone people always tried to say nice things like, she's in a better place, or her suffering is over. They said she was looking down at us from Heaven."

She wiped her eyes, sniffed. "Did that make you feel better?"

"Nope."

"What did?"

"You want the truth?"

"Yes."

"I finally realized she was as sad as me that she had to leave."

"Do you think my mommy is as sad as me?"

"If she isn't, she will be."

"Will she come back?"

"Truth?"

"Truth."

"I don't know."

"Why did she leave?"

"I'd like to be able to say you'll understand when you get older, but we might never know. All I know is that it was wrong of her to leave."

"Papa says you have trouble with right and wrong."

"I suppose I do."

Her mouth was seized by a violent yawn.

"Sounds like you could use some shut eye."

"Will you sit in my room until I fall asleep?"

He picked up his gun. "I'll sit as long as you want me to." He kissed the top of her head. "Get along, little doggie."

She took his hand and led him down the hall to his childhood bedroom. He sat in a comfortable chair in the corner.

"Good night, Uncle Ryan."

"Good night, Cass."

She drifted off quickly. Eventually, Ryan dozed. His mother waited for him in his dreams.

25

It was still dark when Bill left his motel.

The moon was a glowing socket carved out of the blackness. The stars pierced the sky in a dizzying, infinite stretch. He didn't know the constellations any more than he knew Greek. He knew the big dipper but couldn't find it tonight. How could that be?

He was grateful to get inside his rental car. The dashboard lights were a relief, their order and neatness. Every light had a place and a purpose. The weapons were stored in the way back of the station wagon, cleaned, oiled, and loaded.

He looked like a new man. Cargo shorts and hiking boots. A fleece pullover on top of a Yosemite National Park t-shirt. He looked the part but doubted he could carry on a conversation about camping or hiking. He'd never spent a night out under the stars in his life. Of course his face generally cut conversations short.

No service on his phone. He relied on a map he bought at a gas station around the corner.

He turned the car on to the road and couldn't fight the sensation of being a lone astronaut traveling on the surface of some distant planet or moon. He wondered how people kept from going crazy out here. Maybe they were all crazy.

On the outskirts of a place called Arizona City, Bill found the corner he'd been told to meet at. He pulled over, put on his hazards.

A shadow turned into a man's silhouette and walked toward the car. The passenger door opened. A man dressed a lot like Bill got in, with a backpack on his lap. He shut the door.

Bill turned off the hazards and pulled back on to the road.

"Hello, Bill."

"Rico."

"Long time."

Bill nodded. "Thanks for helping me out."

Other than some gray at the temples, some wrinkles around his eyes, Rico looked the same.

Bill handed him an envelope.

"You're the one helping me out, Bill."

They were on the highway now. Just before the turn onto Interstate 8.

"Where we headed?"

"Town called Oscuro. Know it?"

Rico shook his head. "Not much to know about Oscuro County."

They drove in silence. Before long the black sky lightened to gray, then blue as the sun crept above the eastern horizon behind them.

Two hours later, mile after mile, nothing changed. A thin strip of highway surrounded by sand and sky and the ever-present cacti. Occasionally mountains loomed in the distance.

"How do you stand it out here?"

Rico considered. "It's a good place to hide. All this vastness. Good place to just get lost."

They stopped for gas in a town called Gila Bend. They passed a sign that read:

GILA BEND
WELCOMES YOU
HOME of 1700 *Friendly* PEOPLE
And 5 OLD CRABS
Elev 737 ft

Bill couldn't believe 1700 people lived here. Rico used the bathroom, got a bottle of water and some beef jerky. He did some stretching for his back before he got back in the car.

"How long until California?" Bill asked.

"Maybe an hour. Maybe another hour after that to Oscuro."

"It's gotta be a hundred degrees out here."

"Give or take. It don't get hot in Miami no more?"

"Not this hot."

Rico shrugged. Resigned to the heat, to everything the world cared to dish out. Bill observed Rico's left arm, swirls of red and pink where the burns had healed from his wrist up past his sleeve. Bill remembered when they were fresh. Remembered the smell, like meat left too long on the grill. He knew that those scars went past his shoulder. He could have died. But Rico was a tough, stubborn bastard back then. Bill hoped he still was.

Bill wondered if Rico was startled every morning when he looked in the mirror and was reminded of them. Like Bill was. His reflection haunted him like a ghost. He rarely looked at it squarely, resented the creature he'd become.

They crossed the border of California just past the brief civilization of Yuma. The desert quickly reasserted itself. An hour later they drove through the imposing Oscuro Mountain range, finally passing a sign for the town of Oscuro, California. Population: 897.

Three Js was at his desk, reading the paper when he heard the door to the station open.

A man in an Arizona Diamondbacks baseball cap entered. A hiker, was Three Js' first impression.

"Excuse me," Bill said.

The man's left eye didn't follow the right. The skin around the socket was shiny, like wax.

"Can I help you, sir?" Three Js was on his feet. The man smiled. His teeth were perfect.

Bill's one good eye scanned the station, landed

briefly on Teddy McCarthy, but didn't react. Teddy stared at Bill from his cell. "I hope so. I'm looking for the state park."

"The Kumeyaay Forest?"

Bill nodded. "Think you could point me in the right direction?"

"Sure. Take the Old Road out of town. Maybe three miles you'll see a sign for the Kumeyaay Highway. That'll take you right to the front gate."

"Much obliged, Officer." He tipped his cap.

"My pleasure."

"Say. Anywhere you could recommend for a bite to eat?"

"La Cocina. Couple doors down. They'll take good care of you."

"Appreciate it."

Three Js watched him exit, go to his car, and get in. He automatically noted the license plate, make, and model. He wrote it down on a legal pad.

"Notice anything odd about him, Officer Jimenez?"

"Besides the eye?"

"Besides the eye."

Three Js thought about the man, the way his good eye roamed everywhere, taking notes. Then he thought about what the man wore. "Brand new boots. Brand new everything."

"You're a smart hombre. Want some friendly advice?"

He really didn't. But he said, "What's that, amigo?"

"Get the hell out of town."

Three Js looked skeptically at his prisoner.

"That man's name is Bill Glenny."

"Like your name is Virgil Smith?"

"In Miami, they call him Wicked Bill. And you don't want anything to do with him."

"Is that a fact?"

"That's a fact."

1980

In May of 1980, Miami, Florida was an ugly place. Teddy remembered it well. Don Palermo was just Nick Palermo, a tough young boss trying to make a name for himself. And the city was a powder keg that had just caught a spark after the McDuffie verdict.

He'd been in Florida for a year. Teddy had pulled a job up north and needed to get the hell out of Dodge so Benito Gallo had loaned him to the Miami branch of the family. Palm trees, white sand beaches, no snow. Teddy had been happy to leave. Moved his mother down to Fort Lauderdale.

He liked Nick Palermo. An intelligence in his eyes that reminded him of Mr. Gallo. Mixed with a coldness that said Palermo would do what he needed to do.

Teddy had done a few muscle jobs for him. They'd gone well. Teddy's reputation was solid, he was cool under fire, a professional. When somebody said we need a pro, they called Teddy.

Bill Glenny was Palermo's right-hand man, his lieutenant. His reputation was well known. He liked to kill people, but he liked to hurt them even more. Maybe a little too much. No qualms about women and children as targets. No qualms about anything. If you wanted to send a message, you called Bill Glenny.

Teddy knew, in this life, you ran into evil people. Psychopaths, sociopaths. Where else were they gonna go? Some jobs almost required them, if used properly. He'd known some up north. Men with their own code of conduct, men willing to cross any line, men who savored the pain of their victims.

They made him nervous but they were a fact of life.

At that time, Palermo lived in Coral Gables. Nice place. Maybe four or five thousand square feet. Lush, well-manicured lawn, white columns in front.

Teddy knocked on the front door.

A kid answered. Maybe sixteen or seventeen, Teddy had seen him around. What was his name? Rico. Got ticked off when people assumed he was Cuban. So they called him Rico.

"Hey, Rico."

"Hey. They're back here."

Rico led him down a marble tiled hallway. Paintings on the wall of half-nude women, sort of tasteful. Rico stopped at a doorway and held out his hand. Teddy could hear Palermo talking.

Teddy walked into a large office. Palermo sat on the front of a big oak desk. Bill Glenny sat in a leather chair. He nodded at Ted who nodded back.

"I think you boys know each other," Palermo said.

They did. But had never worked together.

"Have a seat, Teddy."

Teddy sat in the leather chair next to Bill. It was tough to guess Bill's age. Early twenties, Teddy guessed. His skin was smooth, no age lines. But his eyes. Not his eyes, maybe just his expression. The dead stare. No reaction. Teddy realized he was the oldest man in the room. When had that happened? He'd been the kid for so long. Now he was the cagey veteran.

"Drink?"

"Take a Jameson's if you got it. Some ice."

Palermo waved at Rico who nodded and went to make the drink.

"What's up?" Teddy said.

Palermo rubbed a hand down his face. "I guess you'd call it a territorial dispute. Some new player in town. Cuban asshole, Martez. Señor Martez is moving into Overtown. Doing some dealing, running some numbers. This cannot be tolerated."

"What's the play?" Teddy asked.

Palermo smiled. "All business. I like that. The play is we send a message. Loud and clear."

They would deliver the message to Martez in person, at his home in Little Havana. Ideally when his whole family was there. Teddy kept his face passive when he heard about the family. But he didn't like it. Maybe Palermo sensed it.

"I trust Bill to do what needs to be done. Teddy, you're there to make sure it goes down smooth. No witnesses. No complications. Like always."

Teddy nodded.

Bill just breathed.

"We could use a driver," Teddy said.

Palermo winced.

"Frees me up to be wherever I need to be. Makes the getaway that much quicker."

"What about the kid?" Bill's voice was much deeper than Teddy expected.

Rico entered and handed Teddy his drink.

"Does he know how to drive?" Teddy asked.

"Rico, how would you feel about chauffeuring these two outlaws around tonight?"

He raised his eyebrows, shrugged.

"You can drive, right?"

That got a smile out of Rico. He thinks it's all fun and games, Teddy thought. Poor kid.

They drove around the block a few times first. The house was tucked into a quiet neighborhood. The family sitting down to dinner. Two dudes in front casually smoking cigars at a table, guns in shoulder holsters. One guy in back listening to some Spanish music on a portable radio.

Simple.

They parked next to a palm tree half a block

away, as far from a streetlight as they could get.

Teddy screwed a silencer onto his pistol.

"Hey, kid."

Rico looked at him with eager eyes.

"Keep the engine on and your eyes open. You wait for both of us then you drive away nice and easy. Don't speed. We don't want the attention. Somebody asks you what you're doing, what do you say?"

"I'm picking up a friend."

"That's right."

Didn't hurt, in this neighborhood, that Rico could pass for Cuban.

"I'll take the front, you take the back?"

Bill nodded.

They split up. In the distance, Teddy heard sirens. Maybe a fire? Plenty of trees to use for cover as he snuck up to the front porch. Two pops. Two men down. Teddy picked up their cigars. He put the first one out in the ashtray. The second one he sampled. He peeked inside. The Martez family carried on as though nothing had happened.

One of the men moaned, turned over. Teddy fired again.

Teddy looked back inside. Bill there now, pointing his gun. Moving it from kid to kid, then to the mother, then pointed it at Martez whose neck bulged, face red. Bill's sleepy eyes were wide awake. A whisper of a smile on his face.

Martez said something Teddy couldn't make out.

Spittle flew from his furious mouth.

Bill shot him in the heart.

The children's eyes bulged. Two boys, the older one twelve, the younger eight or nine, and a little girl of five or six. The girl started to wail. Her hair was long and thick, very curly. She had round cheeks and big, scared eyes.

Their mother tried to keep it together. She said something, appearing calm, but tears squeezed out of the corners of her eyes, down her pretty cheeks. The poor woman thought she was dealing with a reasonable man.

A knife in Bill's hand.

Run, Teddy wanted to tell the children. But they were frozen, mouths gaping.

Bill approached Mrs. Martez, a disarming smile on his face. He brought the sharp knife close to her face and went to work.

Teddy walked to the edge of the front patio and vomited over the side as quietly as he could. Couldn't remember the last time he'd thrown up, the last time something had disturbed him like this. He'd seen some sick shit over the years. Hell, he'd done plenty of sick shit over the years. He spit into some azalea bushes, the burn of bile still strong in his throat, in his nose. This was a whole other level of bad.

The sirens were louder now. Had to be for Teddy to hear them over the blood pounding in his ears.

He looked back inside. He'd hoped Bill had

spared the little girl. Should have known better.

A ghoulish scene, Bill had propped the family at the table, all holding hands as though at prayer. Some instinct made Teddy cross himself. Bill looked like a host making finishing touches before his guests arrived, or a child arranging dolls.

On the patio, Teddy noticed a bottle of rum on a table. He took a big sip, swished it around in his mouth, and swallowed. Did it again. Then he walked to the car where a jumpy Rico waited.

"Is it done?"

Teddy nodded.

"Where's Bill?"

"Just tidying up."

"Was it bad?"

Teddy watched Bill walk out the front door. He straightened his shirt, tucked his gun in the back of his pants.

"It wasn't good, kid."

Bill sat in the back seat. His eyes were flat again, sleepy, his expression bored.

"Take the long way home, Rico. Cut through Overtown."

Teddy could sense Bill's gaze on the back of his head. He didn't want to acknowledge it. He was tempted to light a cigarette but couldn't trust his hands not to shake.

"You think I went too far?"

"I think the message was delivered. Loud and clear."

Bill smiled. "You didn't answer my question."

"I guess I didn't."

The smell of smoke in the car. Emergency lights flashed ahead. Still a fire?

"You think there are rules for what we do?"

"Keep it slow, Rico." He turned to Bill. "What is it you want to ask, Bill?"

He showed some teeth at that. "I think you disapprove of what went down back there. I think you're judging me."

"What's it matter, what I think? What anybody thinks?" He was genuinely curious now.

"You don't take any pleasure in what you do? In hurting people. Or worse."

Teddy thought back to that first time. As a kid. The sound of wood on bone still fresh in his mind. He remembered how it felt, like it had just happened. A lot of fear. A lot of adrenaline. But there had been pleasure. Mixed with relief. Since then, less and less fear. More satisfaction at a well-done task or the buzz when things got complicated, when he had to improvise. There was pleasure there. In the action.

"When they deserve it."

A sneer on Bill's face when he repeated the word. "Deserve? That's a word you should remove from your vocabulary." Bill chuckled.

Ahead of them, brake lights bloomed, cars skidded to a halt. Rico stepped on the brakes. People were moving into the street.

"What the fuck?" Teddy said.

"You better hope you never get what you deserve, Teddy McCarthy."

It didn't make sense. He saw torch flames coming nearer. The mob chanted something. The car was surrounded. Palms pressed against the windows. The car began to rock back and forth. Bill drew his pistol. He fired through the back passenger window. Screams. The mob contorted. Bill fired again. The window shattered. A flaming bottle was thrown inside the car. It hit Bill's head and exploded.

The car was heaved onto its side. Flames. Everywhere.

Bill screamed. They all screamed.

Teddy flipped his door up, climbed out, pulled Rico behind him. Bill still in the back seat.

Screaming.

Rico shook loose of Teddy's grip, ran back to the car, opened the rear passenger door. Reached in and somehow his hand found Bill's. He strained as he yanked him out of the burning vehicle. Bill's face in flames. Rico's right side too.

Both screaming.

Teddy pulled off his shirt. He knocked Rico and Bill down. "Roll, Rico! Roll to put out the fire."

Rico rolled.

Teddy put his shirt on Bill's face, gagged at the smell of cooked flesh. He patted him down to put out the flames. His skin still smoking. So hopped up on adrenaline he barely noticed the ambulance or the EMTs as they arrived and rushed to help. Barely noticed the burns on his hands.

2012

Teddy rubbed his palms together as he remembered the sting of those burns.

"Tell you what, Officer Jimenez. Why don't you get the sheriff on the horn. Tell him about our visitor."

"Bill Glenny."

"Wicked Bill."

26

It was still early when Leo returned home.

Ryan was on the front porch, shotgun on his lap, smile on his face.

"All quiet?"

"All quiet."

"Teddy thought I was going to kill him once he realized I knew who he was."

Ryan nodded. "He knows how things work."

Leo shook his head. "That's how things work in your world? A job goes south, people have to die?"

"Sometimes."

"Jesus."

"I got a pot of coffee going in the kitchen."

Leo walked inside, found a mug. Listened for signs of Cass being awake. Silence. He was tired and the smell of coffee as he poured it had a magic effect. He took a sip, went back outside.

They sat for a bit. The porch was built for sunsets, so the sun rose out of sight behind the house, the sky in front of them gradually deepened its shades of blue.

"Mom used to have her morning cup out here."

Leo thought of the woman from the pictures in the house, the thin young bride, holding a mug in two hands.

"Sometimes I'd wake up early and call for her." His face looked years younger. "I'm just taking a moment, son, she'd say. You'll be okay for a minute." Ryan sipped his coffee. "I'd forgotten all about that."

Leo let him alone with the memory for a few minutes.

"Why did you kill those men at The Cave?" All those years and he'd never asked the question before.

The hard years came back to Ryan's face or maybe it was just getting brighter. "They were in the wrong place at the wrong time. So was I."

"Did it have something to do with Dad?"

His brother's sharp look told him he'd struck a nerve.

The phone rang. Once. Twice.

"You gonna get that?"

After the third ring Leo went inside to answer it, limping on his trick leg.

It was Three Js.

"What's up?"

"Sorry, boss. Just had a bad feeling."

"Why?"

"Guy was just here. Looked like a hiker. Just came in and asked for directions, but there was something off about him."

"You got a hunch?"

"I know. The prisoner claimed to know him. Said the dude's name was Bill. The guy had bad burn scars on his face."

That sent a chill up Leo's spine.

"Mean anything to you?"

"Maybe. Deputy, I want you to be real careful about who comes in and who goes out of the station. Comprendes?"

"Comprendo. What's going on?"

"Our prisoner might be more trouble than he's worth. I'm gonna check on a few things. You let me know if anything weird happens."

"You got it."

"Thee Js?"

"Yeah?"

"Anything."

"Understood."

27

La Cocina was just up Main Street from the police station. Breakfast smells emanated onto the side-walk: eggs, bacon, coffee. The interior was a little worn, a bit shabby, but because of the crowd seemed more like a well-loved toy than a neglected one.

Bill and Rico sat toward the back, away from the large windows in front with a view across the street of the abandoned hardware store. Next to that a barber shop with a red, white, and blue spinning pole out front. Bill stared at it as he thought.

It was fairly crowded and the waitress apolo-gized when she got to the table to refill their cof-fees.

"Busy today," Bill said.

"With Sally's closed we're the only game in town for breakfast."

"Sally's." Bill pretended to remember. "What happened to Sally's?"

The waitress crossed herself. "Terrible. Some bastard came in and shot that poor old man."

"You don't say. Anybody else get hurt?"

"Poor Doris. I heard she saw the whole thing."

"Doris. That isn't Doris Kennedy by any chance is it?"

The waitress shook her head. "No, sir. Doris Farley, I believe."

"Doris Farley."

"You fellas know what you want?"

"I'll have the number two, over easy please."

Rico looked up at her. "Pancakes, por favor."

"No problema, señor."

When the food arrived, Bill said, "You wouldn't be able to put your hands on a phone book would you, dear?"

"I just might."

Bill watched Rico shovel pancakes into his mouth. "What are you, twelve?"

Rico licked his lips and shrugged. Took another bite.

The boyish look on Rico's face took Bill back decades. His old apartment in Miami. An unexpected knock. He answered the door with a gun in his hand. Safety off, ready for business. A scared look on a teenage Rico's wide-eyed face.

Bill wasn't in the habit of accepting guests into his home. If the boy hadn't saved his life, Bill would have laughed and slammed the door in his face. But Rico had, so Bill invited him in. Both of their burns were still fresh, their dreams still vivid. Neither would ever go away, only fade with time.

Bill closed the door and fetched a few stiff drinks. Whiskey.

Rico shook his head.

Bill insisted. "Drink it, kid."

The first sip made Rico cough. His second went smoother.

Bill leaned back in his leather recliner. Rico sat on the couch with his elbows on his knees, held his glass with two hands as if it were keeping him warm. Bill tried to remember the last time someone had sat there. Couldn't.

"What's up, amigo?"

"Cops at my apartment."

Bill fixed Rico with his meanest stare. "They follow you?"

"No."

"You better pray they didn't."

Rico took a sip and winced. "I want out."

"You want out."

"Yes."

"Out of what?"

"This life."

Bill took another sip. Licked his lips. Looked at the burns on Rico's arms. "Why come to me?"

Rico wouldn't look him in the eye.

Bill clicked his tongue. "Because I owe you?"

Finally, Rico looked up.

Bill stood, walked into his kitchen. Found a pen and a piece of paper. "How are you sleeping?"

"I'm not."

"Best way to avoid the nightmares."

"I have two."

Bill wrote down an address. "One where you get burned all over again."

"And one where I don't."

"Hard to say which is worse."

"Waking up is the worst."

Bill handed him the piece of paper. "You go here. You mention my name. They'll fix you up with a new ID. Driver's license, social security card, the whole nine yards."

Rico stared at the address.

"Once you get settled, you send me a postcard with your address on it."

"Why?"

"You never know when I might need a favor."

Rico digested this.

"Don't make me come hunt you down, kid."

He didn't. A few months later a postcard arrived with a picture of the Alamo on it. Bill sent him a thousand dollars for following instructions and to encourage staying in touch. Rico moved every year or two—Texas, Arizona, California, always a small town out west. A place nobody would look for him.

After Ryan Murphy visited Don Palermo, Bill sent a burner phone to Rico with a note: *Be ready*.

When the waitress brought the phone book Bill smiled and said, "Thank you, kindly."

His fingers stopped at her name. "Doris Farley. Hello there." He took a pen out of his pocket. Wrote the address down on a napkin.

Rico raised his eyebrows in a question.

"Let's go see where this Doris lives."

Bill and Rico had just entered La Cocina when Leo asked Ryan, "What would you do?"

"What he's doing. He scoped out the jail. Saw how you had Teddy."

"Now what?"

"He needs to find the waitress."

"Is he going to be able to do that?"

"Probably. It's no secret what happened at Sally's. I'm sure people are talking. He goes to a gas station or restaurant, won't be hard to find out there's a waitress named Doris that was there."

"Shit."

"Bill gets his hands on a phone book he'll know where she lives. Where you live for that matter."

"Why would he want to know that?"

"Give him options. He has trouble finding Doris or doesn't feel like storming the jail, he finds another way to attack the problem."

"It's a hell of a world you live in, brother."

"It's the same one you've always lived in. Now you know where more of the snakes are."

"Thanks for bringing them to my backyard."

Ryan didn't have an answer for that.

28

Doris woke, sitting on her couch, her rifle across her lap, half empty bottle of gin on the coffee table in front of her, a head full of angry bees buzzing. A groan escaped her mouth when she stood and walked on shaky legs to the bathroom. She splashed water on her face, drank some, then threw it up in the toilet. Been a while since she'd had a hangover this bad. In the mirror her reflection shook her head at her. She splashed more water on her face and brushed her teeth.

In her bedroom she changed her clothes.

There was a ridge not far from her house that Doris liked to walk to when she needed to clear her head from time to time. She preferred it at night but she needed to get outside, get some fresh air. So she packed a lunch, peanut butter and jelly and some nuts, and plenty of water. She put on some hiking boots and a good cowboy hat and set out with her rifle over her shoulder into the brutal, blue-skied desert in front of her.

Her headache got worse as she walked, the scent

of gin as she perspired. She kept walking. Uphill, drinking water. The unblinking sun felt a few feet overhead. It was good to be moving, even with no destination. Better than sitting around her house.

Before too long she reached the crest of the hill. A tall desert willow waited for her there. In its shade was a perfect stone for sitting. She sipped her water and wiped the sweat off her forehead with the handkerchief tied around her neck. The sweet scent of the tree's flowers soothed her. The buds about to burst resembled puckered lips about to kiss.

Maybe she just had kissing on her brain. Her tender parts reminded her of her recent encounter with the sheriff. A grin flashed across her face. He looked as good out of uniform as he did in it. Long and lean. And the sex had been fine. Better than fine. She was optimistic that it would get better with practice. She was willing to give it a try.

Sure, he was older. And he had a daughter. Hey, nobody was perfect. She sure as hell wasn't.

Like a lot of residents of Oscuro County, Doris had arrived not looking for anything but running from something. A man. A past. Something about Oscuro had struck her as familiar. She'd grown up in another sandy little nothing of a mining village outside of Odessa, Texas. A town of sun and wind populated by oil men in the employ of Weatherford International. Her father was one of them. Foreman of a group of wells that sucked black gold out of the ground. Her mother had taught third grade for forever. Now she was teaching the kids of her old students.

She missed them. Owed them a phone call. She didn't miss her hometown. Didn't miss her husband. Didn't owe him a goddamned thing.

Maybe it was time to move on. She'd stayed in Oscuro longer than she'd ever planned to. She worried that the longer she stayed in one place, the easier it would be for someone to find her.

She took another sip of water. Looked at her cul de sac in the distance. Nothing moved in the heat. Just a wicked breeze that rustled the branches of the tough trees and bushes that grew in this vicious landscape.

Now she thought about Sal. Tried to think about his kindnesses over the past few years. Somebody in town mentioned that Sal might be looking for some help. A long drive out to that old airstream trailer. She didn't have much experience, she told him, any in fact, just really needed the job. And could they maybe keep her employment off the books?

"Desperate," he'd said. His smile, the glint in his eyes, spoke of his past. "Be here tomorrow at six. We'll see how it goes. I'm a little desperate myself."

Now he was in the morgue, probably being poked at by Dr. Becker. When she'd found him there'd been no thought of saving him, resuscitating him. The memory made her shiver despite the heat. All that blood. She'd only stared. Helpless.

"You could live to be a thousand, Doris," he

liked to tell her when she screwed up an order, "and you couldn't come close to making the mistakes I've made."

She'd thought he was exaggerating. To make her feel better. He rarely talked about his past. Occasionally a detail would slip—about Miami Beach or Florida alligators—and Sal would wince with regret. At the memory itself or the revelation she never knew. She never pressed him.

Had he deserved the fate she'd witnessed? She realized she had no idea.

A truck appeared. She didn't recognize it. Unusual. Not much reason to be in this part of town. It wasn't on the way anywhere. Could be a lost tourist on their way to the national park—that was an easy turn to miss. Something made her doubt it. The truck moved slow. A Chevy pickup.

When it pulled onto her street, she carefully moved into a low crouch and backed up behind the trunk of the desert willow. She held the cool barrel of the rifle in her fist.

She was done being surprised.

As she knew it would, the Chevy came to a stop in front of her house.

Another chill as she watched the driver's door open. A man dressed very much like a lost hiker walked to her front door. He'd left his vehicle running, she saw exhaust coming out of the tailpipe. Too far to hear the engine. Still, she kept her breathing quiet. Wished she could see his face. The hat and sunglasses didn't help.

He peeked into her windows, did a complete loop around her house.

She looked at her neighbors' houses. Everything was still, shades drawn. Please don't come outside, Mrs. Delgado, she prayed to herself. A gasp escaped her mouth when she saw the man get her back door open and walk inside.

Son of a bitch. She squeezed the rifle tighter. Furious. What would he find? The unmade bed, the smell of sex on the sheets. A growl from deep in her throat. She fought the urge to rush down, gun blazing.

Then the man came out the back door, closed it behind him. He stopped and stared right in her direction. Her teeth chattered. Without binoculars he wouldn't be able to discern her from the tree. Would he notice her dirt prints in the sand? Was he some sort of tracker?

Behind her was nothing. Flat desert for miles. Nowhere to run. If the man started up the ridge there was only one thing to do. Shoot first. Ask questions later. Who said things like that? She'd wandered into a Western novel. High Noon. Rio Lobo.

The man stood and stared for a good five minutes, head turning left to right, scanning the ridge.

She didn't move.

Finally he turned back to her house for a moment and went back to the pickup. Another five minutes before the truck pulled away and went back in the direction it came from.

Only when it was out of sight did she stand and head back toward her house, eyes constantly checking the road where the truck might reappear.

As she walked, different scenarios played out in her head. What if she'd been home, sleeping the hangover off instead of sweating it out? What if Leo had been there? Alternating with these thoughts, the image of Sal, shot to death on the floor of the diner.

She wished she'd been closer, that she'd been able to see his face, but knew if she'd been closer he'd have seen her. How could she come this close to death twice in two days?

Inside her house she looked for signs of the man. There was nothing. No stray footprint. No scent of him in the air. Nothing.

She wanted to shower, rinse the salty sweat off her body, but didn't feel safe here. She needed to find Leo. To warn him. And she wanted to do it in person. It felt strange placing the rifle on the floor of the passenger seat of her car, easily reached if necessary. Her tiles squealed as she pulled out of her driveway.

29

Three Js sat at his desk and thought of his father's hometown, Empalme, Sonora. A small city on the coast of the Gulf of California. Views of the water and miles of unspoiled, undeveloped beaches. Generations of struggling farmers and fishermen. A railroad company was the largest employer. His grandfather had wanted more. Like thousands of others, he headed north. He eventually found work in the Murphy Mercury Mine. The work had almost certainly killed him.

But before it killed him, the job paid pretty well, under the table, in cash. A compound of sorts was built around the mine. Old man Murphy built apartments for his employees. Over time, he'd learned that illegal Mexicans, like white men, were more productive with decent roofs over their heads and running water. His competitors would say he spoiled them. Hardly. But he realized that if he retained the same workers rather than having them leave as soon as they could afford to, he saved money training new staff.

Three Js' grandparents spent the fifties in Oscuro. His grandfather underground five or six days a week. His grandmother missed the coast every day. Missed the cool breezes off the water, missed seafood. Here in Oscuro, the stiff breezes were like furnace blasts and Dios mio, was it dark at night. After ten years of exposure to cinnabar, muscles going weak, he let her convince him to return home. A year later, they had a son. Three Js' father.

Juan Jimenez would feel the pull of El Norte too. His mother told him about the tunnel that led to the old mine, abandoned years ago, but maybe the Murphys still had a need for Mexican labor. It was the safest way she knew of to cross the border. Juan had turned sixteen the day before when he loaded a backpack and caught a train north as far as he could, then hitchhiked and walked to San Polvo.

Even knowing where it was, it was difficult to find the tunnel entrance, located now in a forbidding, decrepit corner of the town. His mother told him it would take courage to make it through the passage. He knew it wouldn't be easy. He didn't know it would be so hard. If he hadn't known his parents had survived the journey he might have lost his nerve. But he emerged, hours later, disoriented and tired, in the USA.

At his mother's suggestion, he headed south toward town and, he hoped, work. He tried to make his water last but the sun was merciless and he was so thirsty. The dirt road he followed was barely that, a slight path through the desert almost as rocky as the land on either side. Only a few tire tracks suggested it had ever been used.

Then a flash of steel in the sunlight. An old Chevy approached. Juan considered hiding. But where? The handful of trees were thin as skeletons. He braced himself and waited in plain sight. The rusty pickup bumped along then stopped in front of him. A man in a khaki uniform was behind the wheel. A badge on his chest and mirror sunglasses shone in the sun. Too young to be the Murphy his mother described.

His elbow stuck out the open window. A country and Western song played on the car radio. "Help you?"

Juan took a breath. "Trabaja. Necesito trabaja."

Jeremiah Murphy spit. "Work, huh? Mine closed a long time ago, chico. La mina esta cerrado. Entiendes?"

Juan winced but nodded.

"Wait a minute." Jeremiah removed his sunglasses. Squinted at Juan. "Do I know you? Sé que tu?"

"Maybe my father."

"Jimenez?"

"Sí."

"I'll be damned. You his son?"

"Sí."

"Your father was a good man. I remember your mother too. How are they?"

"My father died a few years ago. My mother is well."

Jeremiah removed his hat. "Sorry to hear about your old man." He sighed. "Why don't you get in."

Juan was too relieved to be nervous. He put his bag on his lap when he sat and shut the door.

"There's not as much work as their used to be. Come te llamas?"

"Juan."

"Juan Jimenez?"

Juan nodded.

"Okay JJ. There is some work. I have a few guys maintain the property. Mend fences, mow lawns, plant bushes. That sort of work. Interested?"

"Yes sir."

"Good."

Jeremiah drove Juan to the Mexican part of town, populated by trailers, a few derelict houses, and a couple of raggedy apartment buildings. He stopped in front of a house that had once been white, now faded to the color of sand by the sun.

"Bring your bag."

Jeremiah introduced him to a kind old Mexican woman named Isabel.

"A truck will meet you at dawn out front. Take you to the ranch." Jeremiah handed him some bills. "Get some dinner. We'll feed you breakfast. You get paid on Friday. See you in the morning, JJ."

Three Js heard this story often over the years. How Jeremiah Murphy had taken pity on his father.

How he'd been patient with the boy because his father had been such a valuable worker. The other members of the grounds crew came and left, rarely stayed more than a season.

Claudia Luna was much more secretive about her past. She was born in Guatemala and left during one of the interminable coups to escape the slaughter taking place in the countryside. She never spoke of what happened to her family, her parents or her older sister. Did they escape with her? Were they victims of the guerrillas? She would only shake her head. One way or another she eventually found herself in Oscuro County cleaning houses with other young girls. She knew of worse fates.

She was cleaning the Murphy house when Juan first saw her. A beautiful young girl with heavy Mayan features, dark hair and eyes, a broad nose and thick lips that never smiled.

One day Claudia was beating a rug outside. Sand was her constant enemy. Juan was having a drink of water in the shade of the house. She hadn't noticed him watching her.

"You never smile."

She gasped and whipped her head to see who spoke, eyes wild.

Juan held up his hands. "Don't be scared."

"I've met scarier men than you."

Juan nodded and walked closer. "I believe it."

She observed him for a moment, then said, "What do you want?"

"I want to see you smile."

She scowled. "Maybe tomorrow."

"I look forward to it."

She rolled her eyes and turned back to her work. A breeze caught her hair, lifted off her neck. That was when he noticed the scar. It started below her left ear and went under her collar.

The next day, Claudia fetched water from the well. Juan approached slowly, careful not to startle her.

"Is today the day she smiles?"

"I don't think so."

He touched his neck. "What happened here?"

Her expression turned hard. She shook her head.

"Maybe tomorrow?"

He waited for an answer.

Finally she shrugged. "Maybe."

"The scar takes nothing away from your beauty."

He was surprised when her expression turned sad. She looked at the ground. He turned and walked away.

"There are more."

He looked back but she was already carrying the buckets back to the house.

A slow courtship began. The other scars did not stop Juan from pursuing her. They were married in Empalme by Juan's parish priest. Claudia had never seen the ocean before. Juan promised to bring her back someday.

Three Js was born in the bathtub of a tiny

apartment in Beantown. It had all happened too fast. Claudia's water broke and the contractions came too close together. A downstairs neighbor stayed with Claudia while Juan went to fetch Dr. Becker. The doctor showed up just as the baby entered the warm water and Claudia passed out. So did the downstairs neighbor, a sweet old woman named Maria who Three Js was pretty sure still lived in the same apartment.

Dr. Becker cleaned the infant up and Juan and the doctor carried Claudia to their bed. When he weighed and measured the boy, he let out a long whistle. "Eleven pounds. Jesus. No wonder she passed out. Kid's a monster."

Becker had all the birth certificate paperwork with him. Three Js was an American citizen.

"What's the name?"

Three Js remembered the first time he met Jeremiah Murphy. He was on his father's lap as he drove a tractor out of the barn. He remembered being impressed by the sheriff's uniform, the badge, the hat, the sunglasses.

"What's your name, little hombre?"

"Juan Jeremiah Jiménez."

"I like it. Kind of a mouthful though. Think I'll just call you Three Js."

There was one cell that was out of sight of the lobby. Down a hallway, through a door. Three Js couldn't remember the last time it was used. Something made him move the old man there. He wasn't sure if it was for the prisoner's safety or just to get him out of earshot. He was tired of the old man's mouth and he was rattled by the stranger asking for directions.

"I didn't sign up for this."

"Well what did you sign up for?" Mrs. O'Leary asked.

He hadn't realized he'd spoken out loud. Mrs. O'Leary had a brown bag with food from La Cocina. Smelled like a burger and fries.

"What's that?"

"Lunch. For the prisoner. Unless you were planning on starving the man to death."

"I haven't ruled it out."

Mrs. O'Leary tsked him. "So what did you sign up for?"

"I don't know."

"I really want to know."

He sighed. "Parking tickets. Maybe some domestic calls. Protecting women and children from abusive husbands and fathers." A shrug. "Kicking a few of my cousins back over the border."

He thought of his mother's scars. Surprising her once in her bedroom as she was changing. He might have been five. The angry pink lines on her skin. Mrs. O'Leary smiled, not unkindly, at him.

"I didn't sign up for Sally's brains and blood all over the floor. Or strangers casing the station, trying to get at a prisoner."

She rubbed his shoulder. "You hang in there, Deputy Jimenez. It's like my momma used to tell me. God only gives us what we can handle."

"I didn't know I could handle all this."

"You never know. Until you know."

"You know what my mother told me?"

"What?"

"There are bad men in the world."

Mrs. O'Leary touched his arm. "There are good men too."

He nodded.

She looked at the empty cell. "Where's the prisoner?"

"Down in cell three."

"Can't remember the last time that was occupied. Maybe when Jeremiah was sheriff."

She walked down the hallway, leaving the scent of the prisoner's meal to remind Three Js how hungry he was.

Teddy couldn't help but smile when he saw Mrs. O'Leary approach his cell. A paper bag in her hand, wet with grease on the bottom and smelling heavenly. Something in her eyes. Big and pale blue, still a child-like quality there, like she was still eager to see what surprises the world had to show her. She must have been something back in the day.

She was still something.

"Mrs. O'Leary, you're an angel."

Her dimpled cheeks blushed. "I don't know about that." She handed him the bag.

"I know an angel when I see one, Mrs. O'Leary." He removed the food.

"Call me Vanessa."

"Call me Ted."

She raised her eyebrows. "I thought it was Virgil?"

He took a bite of the burger, winked. "I prefer Ted."

"Ted." She spoke the name as if she was tasting it. "Okay."

"How's Deputy Jimenez holding up?"

"He sure has the heebie-jeebies."

Ted chewed and swallowed. "He should."

"Why?"

"'Cause there's a bad man in town."

"Who?"

"Man I used to know. They call him Wicked Bill."

"How do you know?"

"He was in here, pretended he was asking for directions."

She frowned. "That's why he moved you."

"I suspect so."

Those big eyes so wide now. "Is Wicked Bill going to break you out?"

"No, Vanessa. Bill only does one thing. He's pretty good at it too."

"He's here to kill you?"

"And anyone else that could tie me to the scene

of the crime. Or anyone that gets in his way."

"Why?"

"I know too much."

"You don't look like you know too much."

"Lord knows I've seen too much."

"You really killed Sally, didn't you?"

"Sally C was a son of a bitch stool pigeon rat. He got what he deserved."

"You don't think people can change?"

"Do you? Have you known anyone that really changed?"

She thought. "A few. Not many."

"I suppose people can go from bad to worse."

"How did you end up like this?"

"Like what?"

"In jail. Again. For killing somebody."

He wiped his face and hands with a napkin, sighed. "I started young. Too young." He bit a french fry. "I was good at it. Most of them were bad people." His eyes were far away, looking back in time. "Like being a soldier, I guess. You follow orders."

"You never wanted to stop?" Her big eyes looked so sad, so concerned.

"Maybe. Maybe a long time ago. I can't remember. The life. That's what they call it. Maybe because that's how long you're in it."

"Do you have any regrets?"

"A gang of them."

30

Three Js wasn't sure where they came from. He was at his desk, his head in his hands, wondering what the fuck had happened to this town, to this world, when he heard somebody clear their throat.

"Bad day?" The hiker from earlier.

Three Js looked up. Another man with him. Hispanic. Not Mexican. Puerto Rican, he guessed. He lowered his hands.

He didn't notice the pistol in the hiker's hand until he fired it, aiming at the phone on Three Js' desk. He hit it, dead center.

"Keep those hands where we can see them, amigo."

He kept his hands up, elbows on the desk.

Something different about the man's voice now, something sinister. No more Mr. Nice Guy.

"Your prisoner seems to have been moved. Where's he at?"

Three Js was about to speak. The man leaped toward him, gun aimed at his head.

"Stand up."

He did.

"Reach for the ceiling. Rico, disarm him."

The other man took Three Js' belt off, pocketed the 9 mm in the back of his pants. He removed the handcuffs and threw the holster and belt into the now unoccupied cell.

"Hands behind your back."

Three Js did as he was told and the other man, Rico, slapped the cold steel around his wrists until it dug in.

"I do like the sight of a cop in his own cuffs. Now lead the way to my old friend."

Three Js hesitated.

"Amigo, don't get cute. It's no skin off you. Guy's a killer. We're just going to get him out of your hair." He held out his hand. "Vamanos."

Three Js couldn't see any way out of it. He prayed Mrs. O'Leary had snuck out the back door. He led the way down the hallway.

"Haven't had a chance to talk with Teddy in a while. Too bad he fucked this operation up so badly. Probably be a short conversation."

The hallway opened into a dim, square room. To the left was a cell. Identical to the ones in the front of the station.

Three Js turned and froze. "Mrs. O'Leary, you crazy old bird."

The cell door was open. The keys dangled from the lock. The smell of Teddy's meal hung in the air.

The cell was as empty as a wino's stomach.

31

Doris pulled in front of the police station. She didn't see Leo's Explorer where he normally parked it. But she recognized another vehicle—the same brown pickup that had parked in front of her house. A Chevy Silverado. Arizona plates. She found a pen, wrote the plate number down. The truck was empty.

She scanned the street, not positive she would recognize the man up close, but she thought she might. The slow, smooth way he moved. The hair on the back of her neck rose at the thought of seeing him. Would he know her?

Mrs. O'Leary suddenly came into view. Doris was about to get out of her car and approach her when she noticed the man next to her.

He wore the same clothes he was wearing when he shot Sal. The hat was pulled low.

They moved fast to Mrs. O'Leary's car. She took the driver's seat, the old man lay down in the back seat. She kept glancing at the police station. Her expression scared, on the verge of tears. She pulled onto Main Street ignoring stop signs and traffic signals and speed limits.

Something bad was happening.

Doris put the car in gear. She needed to find Leo. She headed to the Murphy ranch as fast as her little shitbox would take her there.

32

Mrs. O'Leary gasped when she heard the gunshot from the front of the station. Teddy put his fries down and wiped his hands with a napkin. She started to walk toward the noise.

"I wouldn't."

"What?"

"Go out the back door, Vanessa."

"But what was that?"

"Bill." He'd bet his life on it.

"That doesn't make any sense."

"I suppose not. Listen, you don't have a lot of time. Deputy Jimenez will buy you what time he can. You need to scram."

She shook her head, eyes welling. "What about you?" She stepped in front of the cell, put her trembling hands on the bars.

"You're awful pretty when you're scared, Vanessa." He put his right hand on her left. "Please get the hell out of here."

A sudden change in her face, her jaw tightened. Her eyes hardened, this close they resembled blue glass marbles. She turned and grabbed the keys then unlocked the cell door.

Teddy had heard people talk about love. You read about it. Saw it in movies. He'd never had much use for it. Just something to complicate his life, he thought. He was a lone wolf, didn't rely on anyone. Didn't want anyone to rely on him. Love was bullshit, he'd always said.

But a weird lump sat in his throat as he watched her stand in front of his cell.

"What are you doing?"

"Rescuing you, dummy."

"I'll be damned."

Now he was in her car, headed west out of town. He could have left her anytime. Overpowered her or just walked away. He doubted she'd put up much of a fight. Probably he should have stolen her car and gotten the hell out of Dodge. For some reason he didn't. Something was throwing his instincts off.

Yesterday, driving through the desert alone, he'd hated it. Found it desolate and sad. Now, with her driving, her scent amplified in the closeness of her car, he was aware of a severe beauty in the landscape.

It felt unreal, dreamlike. The jail cell had been familiar, even the smell of it, the uncomfortable bed. Now hauling ass in this kind woman's car through a world he'd never imagined, like something out of

Lawrence of Arabia, he was disoriented.

They traveled over a ridge and came down into a cluster of small, neat homes on small, neat lots. A charming neighborhood with mature trees and actual lawns. She pulled into the driveway of a gray house with a white picket fence. A brick planter in the front of the house beneath a big bay window was filled with purple and white impatients which threatened to spill over the edges.

"Be quick. My neighbors are all terrible gossips."

They rushed into the house.

Inside, the charm continued. Cozy, was the word that came to Teddy's mind. A room with two comfortable-looking couches and a brown leather chair led to a dining table in front of a sliding door. Tchotchkes everywhere. What looked like Mexican or Native American artwork.

"Make yourself at home. I've got a call to make."

"To who?" he couldn't help asking.

She pointed a stern look in his direction. "I think it's about time you trusted me, Teddy."

In a previous life he might have grabbed her by the throat and squeezed until she told him. In this life, he was about to speak, about to do something he'd regret, but stopped himself and nodded at her.

He walked to the sliding door. A small deck outside with a circular glass table and four chairs. Tall trees provided shade in the backyard. Beyond the fence that marked the end of the property, the desert resumed. Miles and miles of sand until, far away, low on the horizon, stony mountains appeared.

"Glenn, is that you?" She was using a green phone hung on the wall. As she talked she twirled the cord around her finger. Might be the same phone he had in his kitchen as a kid. "I've been better, Sheriff."

Teddy felt an involuntary shiver at her last word.

"All hell's broken loose down here. I'm not gonna beat around the bush. We could use some help."

Teddy fought his instincts. The urge to hang up her phone, rip the cord out of the wall. Tie Vanessa up and leave her in the bedroom. Take whatever cash he could find, take her car. If he could get back to LA he could probably figure something out. Hustle a fake ID. Head to Mexico.

That's what young Teddy would have done, maybe worse. The best witnesses are dead witnesses had always been his motto.

"Thanks, Glenn. I sure appreciate it." She hung up, looked at Teddy. "Cavalry's on the way."

As he watched her, the events of the last hour or so sank in. He wasn't surprised when the tears came. He was surprised when he came close to her. Was shocked when he held his arms open and she allowed him to embrace her.

"Not as tough as you act, are you?"

"What will they do to Three Js?"

He chose not to answer. Nothing good.

She sobbed. He held her tighter.

Bill would use the deputy for information. Find

out where Sheriff Murphy lived. He sucked in his breath.

"What?"

"We need to get you out of here."

"Why?"

"Bill will find out where you live. He'll come looking for me."

She went to the kitchen sink, turned on the water. She splashed some water on her face, toweled it dry. Took a deep breath. Here was that firmness he'd gotten so fond of, that sparkle in her big blue eyes.

"What size pants are you?"

"Thirty-two waist. Thirty-two inseam."

"Close enough." She pointed. "Go take a quick shower. You smell like jail. I'll get you some clothes."

When was the last time he'd been a guest in someone's home? Had to be decades. He still fought that convict's reflex to tense up when he turned the shower on. Once the water was just right, he stepped in and let his mind wander.

He'd been out maybe a week. Staying in some flea-bag motel downtown getting his bearings when Bill came to visit him. Teddy came out of the bathroom after a tepid shower and there was Bill. The burns on his face long healed and waxy.

"Nice place, Teddy."

He shrugged. "I've stayed in worse."

Bill had a thick envelope in his hand. "Palermo

wanted me to give this to you." He threw it on the bed.

"Much obliged."

"He also wanted me to ask what your plans were."

Teddy frowned. "Plans?"

"You know, like what you're doing tomorrow. Or the day after."

"Really hadn't thought that far ahead."

"I get it. Been a while since you needed to make any plans. Since that raw deal you got."

"Yup." Teddy felt a surge of resentment. Bill had been recovering from his injuries when Sally had been fingered and turned into a state witness. Otherwise Bill would have been in the cell next door. Rico too maybe, but he'd bolted town when the word that Sally had turned rat hit the streets.

It must have shown in Teddy's face because Bill turned his face, moved the burned half toward Teddy.

He pointed to it. "You think I got off easy? Care to trade places, handsome?"

Teddy took a deep breath. "I guess we both got raw deals."

"What if I told you there might be a way to settle an old score?"

"I'm listening."

"We got a line on Sally."

This caught Teddy off guard. When he pictured his life after prison, he'd fantasized about finding a quiet town. Maybe in Mexico, or the Caribbean.

Live quietly, cheaply. He realized his hands were fists. "Where is he?"

"Small town in California. Witness protection." Bill stood, pointed to the envelope. "There's a ticket in there. For tomorrow. Get some new threads and a few good meals."

Teddy eyed the envelope. A warmth billowed inside him, a swell of euphoria. The familiar buzz of having somebody to kill. He'd missed it.

"Rental car info's there." Bill checked his watch. "Guy'll be here in an hour or so to take care of a fake ID for you." Bill paused, looked at Teddy. "Assuming you're in. Are you in, Teddy?"

"I'm in."

If a snake could smile, that's what Bill's grin looked like.

He'd regretted that decision ever since they picked him up in the desert. He dried himself off with Vanessa's soft purple towel. He smelled like Ivory soap. His face was clean shaven. Clean as a whistle. Maybe it was all worth it.

She'd put some clothes on the counter. Jeans and a denim button down. Cowboy clothes. The pants were a little wide in the waist, the shirt long in the sleeve. It occurred to him he was wearing a dead man's clothes. That couldn't bode well.

33

In Leo's kitchen, Jeremiah listened to his sons explain the situation they were in. His expression never changed, an aggravated scowl remained firmly in place. When they finished he sipped from his mug of coffee.

Finally he looked at Ryan, "What the fuck is wrong with you, boy?"

Ryan didn't answer, didn't look at his father. Kept his gaze out the window toward the road that led to the ranch.

"Who the fuck makes a living out of people dying?"

"This isn't helping, Dad."

Jeremiah kept his fierce eyes on his oldest son a few moments longer.

The kitchen phone rang. They looked at it like it was a wild animal. Leo answered on the fourth ring.

"Hello?"

"Sheriff Murphy?"

Leo didn't recognize the voice. "Who wants to know?"

"I do, Sheriff. I don't think we've been properly introduced. I know your brother." Leo looked at Ryan. "I don't suppose he's there by any chance?"

Leo tried to control his breathing, didn't want to show any fear. "What do I call you?"

A chuckle. "Well I've been called a lot of things over the years."

"Bill?"

Another chuckle. "I see my reputation precedes me."

"What do you want?"

"I want to clean up the mess your brother made. Same as you. I admit, my methods might differ slightly from yours."

"Slightly?"

"But we want the same thing."

"I doubt that."

"Don't we both want this all to just go away? It's easily done. And you don't really have to do anything. In fact that's just what I want you to do. Nothing. Talking to your brother makes me think you've got a lot of practice looking the other way."

Rage and shame mingled in Leo's heart, turned his face hot. The phone shook in his hand.

"Sorry. Did I hit a nerve? Oh, somebody wants to say hello."

It was difficult to hear over the pounding of blood in his head. Some sort of struggle on the other end of the line. The sound of something being struck, someone crying out in pain. Leo thought he recognized who it was.

Bill's voice said, "Say hello, Deputy."

"Fuck you," Three Js said.

"He's a tough hombre, Sheriff. I would think you'd want to keep him safe. Best way to do that is to sit tight until all this is over. Best way to keep everybody safe. Your father. Your pretty daughter, Cass."

"That a threat?"

"That's a fact. Relax, it'll all be over soon."

The line went dead.

Leo put his fist through the wall next to the phone.

"What'd he want?" Ryan asked.

Leo rubbed his hand, wiggled his fingers. They all worked without too much pain. "He wants me to sit this one out. He's at the jail. He's got Three Js. I can only assume Ted's already dead." Leo had to restrain himself from punching the wall again.

Cass' footsteps from down the hall came closer until she appeared in the doorway. "What the hell's going on?"

"Watch your mouth," Leo said.

"It's not as bad as what Papa says. What happened to the wall?"

"Nothing," Leo said.

"Nothing?"

Leo grabbed his gunbelt, went to his bedroom to get his 9 mm. He had a shotgun in the Explorer.

"Where are you going?" Jeremiah said.

"Into town. I can't leave Three Js there."

Ryan turned from the window. "If he already

took care of Ted, his next stop is the girl's house."

"Doris."

"She's the last loose string."

"What's happening?" Cass said.

"Let's go," Ryan said.

Leo took a breath, closed his eyes, nodded.

"Where are you guys going?"

Leo squeezed her cheeks and kissed her on the forehead. "After some bad guys." He walked outside.

Ryan patted her on the head before he followed his brother.

The sky was thick with clouds. The air steamy. The sun a dim, white circle above them. The brothers didn't speak, just walked to Leo's Explorer and got in. Kept silent as Leo turned the ignition, skidded out of the driveway onto the state road.

Leo's bad leg ached like it usually did before a storm. Perfect, he thought. Just what they needed on top of everything. He headed east toward Doris' house. Couldn't keep images of her being hurt, a gun held to her temple or worse, out of his head.

Felt strange to be driving with Ryan in the car. Felt wrong for some reason.

The further east one looked, the angrier the clouds grew. At the horizon a few jagged lines of lightning. Too distant to hear thunder. For now.

Doris saw the lightning in her rearview mirror. Wouldn't be long before it was on top of them. She hadn't seen a forecast in days. No idea how severe it was supposed to be. The tires squealed as she sped through the twists and turns of Rye Canyon Road.

Finally, the Murphy ranch came into view.

Her heart sank a bit when she didn't see Leo's vehicle. Puzzlement when she saw Ryan's black Jeep. Did Jeremiah buy a new vehicle?

She screeched to a halt in front of the house.

Jeremiah and Cass came out to greet her.

She knew the answer before she asked. "Is Leo here?"

Jeremiah shook his head. His eyes were angry, she wasn't sure why. "You're Doris, pretty lady?"

"Yes."

The old man nodded. "They went to find you."

"They?"

"My daddy and Uncle Ryan."

"I really need to talk to him. Why did they go to find me?"

"Doris, why don't you come in. We've got a lot to talk about."

"But..."

He held up a hand. "I know. There's a bad man out to get you. I think the safest thing might be for you to come on in, my dear."

Her shoulders slumped, her eyes watered.

Jeremiah came closer, put an arm on her shoulder. "Come on. We'll try to get this sorted out."

34

Three Js sat slumped on the bed in the cell that had last been occupied by the old man. Teddy, this man called him. He couldn't ever remember being so scared. His back was soaked with sweat. He tried to stifle the shivers that coursed under his skin.

He'd seen killers before. Men who'd killed their wives in drunken rages, gangbangers after a drug deal had gone sour and a standoff turned into a shootout.

This man was different.

The other killers he'd known—even the old man from today—in their hearts they were ashamed of what they'd done. Somewhere, in their eyes or their posture, or their voice, was regret.

Not this man.

This was a terrible creature he hadn't encountered before. The proverbial stone cold killer.

The man pulled a chair in front of the cell. His partner leaned back in a chair against the far wall. The man with the burned face sat, Three Js couldn't keep from staring at the terrible scars on the left

233

side of his face.

"What's your name, amigo?"

"I'm not your amigo."

Amusement flickered in his good eye. "Not yet. No. Maybe because we haven't been properly introduced. I'm Bill. And you are?"

"Chingado."

The Puerto Rican laughed out loud.

Bill chuckled. "I suppose you are pretty well fucked. Back there, that's Rico."

Rico winked.

"Okay then. Now you know who we are. I'm gonna ask you some questions. But first, Deputy Jimenez, I want you to do some thinking. I see the ring on your finger. So I suppose there's a Mrs. Jimenez waiting at home for you? And if I were a betting man, I'd wager there's a bambino or two, maybe more, waiting with her."

Some of the fear gripping him gave way to anger.

"I've seen that look before, Deputy. On more men's faces than I care to remember. And I'm still breathing. Don't go thinking you're the one that can kill me. Lot of tougher bastards than you thought they could. They couldn't."

Three Js closed his eyes. Pictured his wife and children. When he opened them, Bill's menacing face stared at him.

"Tell me where the sheriff lives, and this Mrs. O'Leary."

He thought of his mother, the terrible story her

scars told. Yet she'd survived her ordeal. "No."

Three Js enjoyed the change in Bill's expression. "No?"

"No way."

Bill looked at Rico, who shrugged. Bill came close to the bars of the cell. "You sure about that?" He pointed his pistol at Three Js.

Three Js closed his eyes again. He let his mind flip through memories, a mental photo album. His wedding, his daughters' birthdays, their first steps. Tried to remember their voices, their scents. The first time he kissed his wife, she couldn't stop giggling. His stubble tickled her, she said. He tried to hold on to these thoughts when the bullet exploded into his left knee. His world turned incandescent with pain. He was consumed by it. There was nothing else. Except Bill's voice.

"Don't worry, amigo. It will only get worse." A blade in his hand.

"You gonna finish him off?"

Bill observed the deputy with a frown on his face.

"Boss?" It was all Rico ever called him.

"What's that?"

"You gonna take care of him?"

Bill savored the suffering noises the deputy made. "He's a tough son of a bitch isn't he?"

Bill crouched, watched the man, who appeared to be trying to keep his insides from leaving his body. Rich, red blood leaked through his fingers.

Rico nodded. "I'll give him that."

Didn't cave to the threat to his family. Loyal to his sheriff. A rare trait. Now he was paying the price. Probably he would bleed out and die. Maybe someone would come by. Bill was tempted to give this tough hombre at least that chance.

See how tough he really was.

Bill folded his knife and tucked it away.

"That's it?" Rico asked.

He nodded. "That's it. We've got Murphy's address. Same with the old lady."

Simple enough. They found an issue of *Guns & Ammo* in a desk with the name Leo Murphy and an address beneath it. Vanessa O'Leary's they found on an old pay stub.

"Teddy won't be there," Rico said.

"Doubt it. Probably Mexico bound by now. Let's go visit the Murphys."

A slight pause caught Bill's attention. He turned to look at Rico.

"I didn't sign on to kill a bunch of cops."

"You can leave any time, Rico."

Rico seemed to think about it.

"You coming?"

35

There was no car in the driveway at Doris' house. The front door was locked.

"Move over," Ryan said. He was able to pop the lock with a credit card.

The house was just as Leo had left it. Lonely pictures on the wall. A quick pang in his chest when he saw the unmade bed. He didn't know if it was good or bad that there was nothing amiss. No sign of a struggle. That was good. He noted her rifle was missing. That was probably bad.

Ryan had stopped to examine the photograph of the San Diablo lights. "Is that...?"

"Yup."

His brother nodded in appreciation.

"Okay. Next stop, the police station."

Before they reached the car, Mrs. Delgado from next door rushed out of her house. The years had turned her hair gray and her still-sharp eyes looked out from a nest of wrinkles.

"Well if it isn't the Murphy boys."

"Mrs. Delgado?"

"Orion Murphy. Aren't you wanted for something?"

"They let me off for time served in your detentions."

She chuckled. "I think you still hold the record." The chuckle turned into a cough. After it passed she said, "Sheriff, somebody else was snooping around this house."

"Who?"

"Strange man, a few hours ago. Searched the house, then left."

"Where was Doris?"

Mrs. Delgado pointed to the land behind the houses. "Sometimes she likes to hike out to the foothills and back. I was going to say something but she left as soon as she got back."

"What did the man look like?"

She held a hand over the left of her face. "Bad burns on this side."

Leo and Ryan shared a look.

"You know him? Is he the one who shot Sally?" Her eyes were wide at the thought.

"He's a bad guy, Mrs. Delgado. You see him again, you lock your doors and give me a call."

"Okay, Sheriff. What if I see Doris?"

"You could tell her I'm looking for her."

"Business or personal?"

Ryan rolled his eyes.

"You take care, Mrs. Delgado."

"How's your father these days?"

"Good afternoon, ma'am."

"You could tell him I'm looking for him." She cackled as they got back into the Explorer.

"Christ," Ryan said. "It was never easy to keep a secret in this town."

They hauled ass to the police station, ignoring every traffic sign on the way.

Ryan was out of Leo's Explorer before it stopped in front of the station. Leo right behind him.

"That's Three Js' cruiser."

They ran inside. The few pedestrians on the street stopped and stared. Hadn't been a scene like this in recent memory. Two murders already today, the Oscuro rumor mill would be turning at full capacity for weeks to come.

Nobody at the desks in front. No prisoner in the cell. Leo's sidearm was drawn. So was Ryan's. Leo sighed. What did it matter at this point? Screw procedure.

"Three Js?"

A weak groan from the back of the station. They moved slowly toward it, eyes alert for any movement. Ready for a trap.

They found him in a fetal position in the back cell. Too much blood, Leo thought as he unlocked the door. He took a knee and put a gentle hand on his deputy's shoulder.

Ryan secured the rest of the station then called, "All clear." His knee was bad. What looked like knife slashes on his stomach. It was hard to find the wounds beneath the blood.

"Where's your first aid supplies?"

"Against the back wall."

"Got it."

Ryan pulled Leo back. "Call 911."

Leo marveled at his brother's calm. He'd seen this before, he realized, in the service. Probably worse. He wrapped the knee with gauze, tore tape off with his mouth.

"Fucking get on the phone."

Leo dialed. "This is Leo Murphy, sheriff of Oscuro."

"What can we do for you, Sheriff?"

"I got an officer down at the police station on Main Street. I need an ambulance ASAP."

"On the way, Sheriff."

"Much obliged."

He called Becker.

"Hey, Beck. I need you to get the fuck over here."

"Another one?"

"Three Js. Shot and stabbed. It's a mess. Still breathing though."

"Christ. I'm on my way."

"Get over here, bro."

Ryan's hands were covered in Three Js' blood. Leo knelt next to him.

"Put pressure right here."

Three Js winced and sucked in a breath.

"You're okay, Deputy," Ryan said. "Hang in there."

"Is he gonna be okay?"

"Don't ever ask that question." Ryan put his face right in front of Three Js. "Look at me, Jimenez. Look at me."

Eyes full of pain and fear.

"You're gonna be okay, you son of a bitch. Hang in there. This is a goddamned paper cut compared to what I've seen."

Hard to tell if that was a grimace or a smile on the deputy's face.

They stayed like that. Leo didn't know how long. He kept pressure on the wound, smelling blood and the alcohol, Ryan used to clean the other wounds. Three Js went in and out of consciousness.

"Wish I had some morphine. You might want to stock some in the future."

"I'll do that."

Becker got there first, eyes bloodshot and reeking of gin. Leo had never been so happy to see his drunk face.

Becker put his bag on the ground. Pulled a stethoscope out, wrapped it around his neck. "Let me see."

Leo got queasy when he saw what was left of the knee.

Becker sighed. "Ambulance on the way?"

A siren in the distance answered his question. Leo nodded.

"Ryan Murphy. How the hell are you?"

"Hello, Doc."

"This is you doing the field dressing?"

"Yup."

"Nice work."

Three Js gasped something. They went silent, waiting for more.

Leo said, "What's that, Three Js?"

"He wanted to know where you lived."

"Who?"

"The man with the burned face."

"Bill," Ryan said.

Three Js nodded.

The ambulance pulled in front of the station.

Three Js slumped back into unconsciousness.

"Sounds like you boys got somewhere to be."

"Take good care of him, Beck."

Then the EMTs stormed in. Becker had orders for them.

36

Jeremiah stood on the porch of his old house looking through a pair of binoculars. He scanned the road in front of him. No sign of activity. Behind him the sun was low on the horizon casting long shadows. Soon he wouldn't be able to see anything that didn't have headlights. He eyed all the ridges in the surrounding landscape. Plenty of places to hide.

The girls were inside. Cassiopeia was trying to figure out what was going on. Why was everyone so tense? Why was Uncle Ryan in town? She was asking all the right questions and sooner or later somebody was going to have to give her some answers.

Once that sun went down, he didn't like his chances.

Morbid thoughts came to him. He thought of all the people who had died in this house. His father, his mother, his wife. He didn't want to add Doris and Cassiopeia to that list.

He'd listened to Doris' story. The man at her house. The same truck at the police station. The call earlier. This sounded like a truly evil man. A rare breed. Most bad guys weren't all bad. There was usually a line they wouldn't cross. Every once in a while you encountered a man with no conscience. Maybe this was one of those men. A special kind of madness.

There was a bank robber years ago. Jeremiah and a young deputy had tracked him to an old girlfriend's house. A shack way out east in the foothills of the Oscuro Mountains. Jeremiah couldn't come up with his name. They found the robber's vehicle hidden in an old barn.

Jeremiah picked the back door's lock. They crept into the house, pistols drawn. They heard a boy playing. The girlfriend's son. A towheaded five-year-old came running into the kitchen with a toy plane in his hand. He was making jet engine noises with his mouth.

When he saw the two policemen in his house he froze. His mouth made a circle as wide as his eyes. Jeremiah was about to put a finger to his lips but the boy turned and ran, hollering, "Hank!" That was the son of a bitch's name.

"Hank, they're here!"

He should have waited. They'd already called in the marshals. Should have just waited for the cavalry to arrive with a hostage negotiator.

Some lessons you learn the hard way.

They pursued. Jeremiah tried to grab the kid, who was part jackrabbit, as he hopped upstairs. Jeremiah got a hand on the boy's wrist but he twisted free and turned left at the top of the steps.

Jeremiah rolled into the hallway. Heard a shot fired. Too high. Came up on one knee, pistol pointed straight ahead. Hank, in boxer shorts and bare-chested, had an arm around the boy's mother's neck, his pistol pressed against her head.

He was boyish and slender with curly blonde hair. His voice was much deeper than Jeremiah expected. "Drop your gun or somebody dies, Officer."

"Don't do anything stupid, son." Jeremiah inched closer, his mind scrambled for a way out of this standoff.

The little boy was in tears. "Mommy. Mommy." He pulled at her hand. "Let my mommy go!"

Jeremiah would never forget the look on Hank's face as he pointed the gun at the boy and pulled the trigger. An icy expression, then a thin smile at Jeremiah. He was about to say something but Jeremiah was shooting by then. Emptied his chamber into Hank's head.

It was a scene out of a slasher movie. The naked woman, covered in blood from Hank and her son. Her banshee wails shook the house.

The deputy vomited in the hallway. It would be his last day on the job. His hand would develop a tremor that never went away. He would take a job as the manager of the general store on Main Street and when he gave you your change back, the coins would jingle in his shaking hand. People swore it got more pronounced when Jeremiah came into the store.

* * *

Thick clouds made for a dim twilight. He searched his barren property again. Had he waited too long? Nearly dark already out there. Fixing to get darker.

Inside Cass and Doris were playing cards.

"I hate to break up the party, ladies."

"What is it, Papa?"

"Once the sun goes down we'll be sitting ducks."

Doris looked out the window. "Getting pretty dark out there."

"Cass, I want you to take the truck and drive to the old mine entrance. This Bill character won't know anything about it."

"What about you, Papa?"

"You're a sweet kid. Don't worry about me. I was chasing bad guys before your daddy was born."

"But these bad guys are chasing you."

Doris shook her head. "No, they're chasing me."

"And they're not going to catch you. It'll be easier if I don't have to worry about you two if the bad guys get here. Let's go."

The sun was an orange ember behind thick clouds low in the sky. A pitch black night on the way. Doris went to her car to fetch her rifle.

Jeremiah admired the confident way she held it as she walked to catch up with him and Cass. He could see what Leo saw in her now. Something deeper than skin. How she carried herself, the way she looked at you. This was not just another pretty face.

They got to the truck.

"Cass will drive. She knows the way."

He handed Cass a pistol. A .38. "The keys are in the ignition." She took the pistol.

"What's the rule about using this on a person?"

"Only if it's them or me."

He pulled her tight and kissed the top of her head. He was reluctant to let her go. Squeezed her once more. "Get along little doggies."

"When do we come back?"

"When me or your dad comes to get you."

Doris put an arm around Cass and they got into the truck. Jeremiah waved to them as Cass revved the engine and pulled away.

He didn't notice the footprints until the truck was out of sight. An odd tread that he didn't recognize. They came from the west, from behind a rocky hill. They vanished where the truck had been parked just moments before.

Fingers of terror slipped into his chest and squeezed his heart.

Then he was in the headlights of a Crown Vic that pulled into the driveway.

37

1994

Glenn was on his way home after a twelve hour day. He looked forward to getting out of his uniform, cracking a Pacifico. Or six. An uneventful day for the most part. A house burglary, a fistfight at the Wagon Wheel bar downtown, a few domestic disputes. Par for the course.

He waved to his neighbor, Ned, as he pulled onto his street. People always felt the need to wave to cops. Parked his cruiser in the garage. As soon as he was out of the vehicle he undid his holster belt and hung it over his shoulder. His hips were raw from its rubbing. He had to look into getting a more comfortable rig. In the kitchen he hung it on a chair back. He flipped the light on and grabbed a cold beer from the fridge.

He sat on the couch, kicked off his boots, and turned on the TV. The Rangers were playing the Angels. Should be a decent game. He put his feet up on the coffee table.

The sound of a round being chambered from be-hind made him choke on a sip of beer. He stood, coughing, painfully aware that his sidearm was ten feet away in the kitchen.

"Hello, Glenn."

"Ryan Murphy. To what do I owe the pleasure?"

A faint smile on Ryan's face. Glenn couldn't help but think of him as a boy. When he'd come upon him fighting back tears in the cab of his father's pickup. Not sure if his little brother was going to live. Now all grown up. Pointing a gun at him.

"Maybe I should just call you El Jefe."

"Sounds like you think you know something. That's a nice pistol. Plan on using it?"

"Not if I don't have to."

Glenn had been shot at before. In the service. A few times by criminals. He couldn't recall having a gun aimed at him like this. Nothing this close, this damned intimate. His life one finger pull from end-ing. He searched Ryan's eyes for a sign of the boy he'd helped years ago. All he saw was hardness.

"The men you sent after my father."

"The what now?"

A grin on Ryan's face, but still the hardness in his eyes. "Play dumb again with me. See what it gets you."

Glenn could see where it would get him. After what seemed like a long time, he blinked and nodded.

"The men you sent after my father."

"The men you killed?"

"You got them killed when you sent them after my father."

Glenn held off answering that.

"I'll chalk that up to a business decision. I haven't forgotten what you did for my brother. But that's it. Your one get out of jail free card. My father's off limits."

"You make a tough offer to refuse."

Ryan was right. It was strictly business. Oscuro was the easiest place to move cargo, human or otherwise, across the border. Not too much federal oversight. Oscuro County was an easy place to forget about, an easy place to be forgotten about in. But Ryan's old man wasn't interested. There was money to be made. Buckets of it. All Jeremiah wanted to do was protect and serve. Eliminate him, Glenn reasoned, and you eliminate the problem.

Now another thought occurred to him. Another way to skin this particular cat.

"You're skipping town, I take it?"

Ryan's expression said, *Maybe, what's it to you?*

Glenn nodded. "Heading south maybe? That's what I'd do. Plenty of desert to disappear in. Do me a favor."

"You want a favor?"

"Once things cool down. Might be I could use a good man south of the border."

Ryan said nothing. Backed out of the kitchen.

"Do we have an agreement?"

"Stay away from Jeremiah, Glenn."

"Doesn't seem to be in my best interest anymore."

A well-trained American soldier with a checkered past on the run from the law. Could be more than useful. Not to mention that maybe he could persuade Jeremiah to play ball. Or eventually his cop son, Leo.

38

2012

Jeremiah watched the police cruiser haul ass up the driveway. TOWN OF QUICKSILVER POLICE was written on the doors. The Crown Vic skidded to a halt in front of him. The glare of the hazy, setting sun made it impossible to see into the driver's window until it rolled down.

Jeremiah wasted no time, moved quickly to the passenger side and got in.

"Let's talk on the way."

"On the way where?"

He pointed east. "Head over to that service road. Probably keep it under fifty. Lots of twists."

Glenn did as he was told.

"What the hell are you doing here, Glenn?"

He wore aviator sunglasses beneath a white cowboy hat. His sheriff's badge reflected what sunlight there was. "Got a frantic call from Mrs. O'Leary. What the fuck's going on down here?"

"A few desperadoes have come into town."

"This have anything to do with the dead Mexican they found out on The Old Road?"

"More than likely."

"Anything to do with your boy?"

"I'm pretty sure one of them desperadoes is in the back of my pickup. My granddaughter and another gal are driving it to the old mine entrance."

"What makes you say that?"

"Set of footprints. They disappear where the truck was parked."

"What other gal?"

"Local girl. Murder witness."

"From Sally's? The waitress?"

"That's the one."

"This way, right?"

"Yup. Keep west. See the tire tracks?"

A well-worn dirt road stretched ahead of them.

"How far ahead of us are they?"

"Five or ten minutes."

Glenn removed his sunglasses. "Gonna be a dark one."

The sky just after sunset was a colorless blank canvas.

"What's this all about? Why are they after you?"

"Not me. Leo's got a prisoner who killed some-body. He must know too much. His boss wants him and all the witnesses in the ground."

"This is the guy who pulled the trigger on Sally?"

"Yup."

"Shame."

"Not really. He was a lowlife government stool pigeon in a previous life."

"Witness protection?"

"You got it."

"How about that."

The road, such as it was, turned rougher. Glenn slowed down. Still no sign of lights ahead.

"Who tipped somebody off to Sally?"

Jeremiah sighed.

"Let me guess. Your oldest?"

"Looks that way."

"Can't blame a guy for trying to make a buck."

"I can. And I do."

Glenn chuckled.

"Something funny?"

"You, Jeremiah. You're funny. Out here in the middle of nowhere. Nobody watching. Christ, God doesn't even know there's people out here. Still Mr. Clean."

It was a conversation they'd had before. Once. Glenn had approached him years ago. Asked him to look the other way for a few bucks. Jeremiah knew Glenn was hardly the only law man along the Mexican border making a profit off the drug trade. Jeremiah just wasn't built that way. He knew intuitively that once you crossed that line, there was no crossing back.

"You know," Jeremiah said. "I always expected a visit from someone. Figured you'd send men with guns to get me out of the way."

That chuckle again. A chuckle that said Glenn knew things Jeremiah didn't. It got under his skin.

"I did send them."

"What?"

Glenn turned to look at him. Both men were clearly surprised.

"He never told you?"

"Who? Told me what?"

"Those two dead Mexicans. Back in '94."

"At The Cave." Jeremiah remembered the bullet wounds in their heads. "Ryan."

"All these years, you thought it was some random violence? Just Ryan blowing off some steam? No wonder that boy turned out the way he did. He saved your ass that day. And you sent him away."

Jeremiah's mouth had gone dry, not a drop of spit left. "Why didn't you ever try again?"

"Your son made it pretty clear what would happen to me if I did."

"He knew it was you?"

"He figured it out. My heart was never really in it. I didn't particularly like you, Jeremiah, but I didn't particularly want you dead, either. Anyway it wasn't long before Ryan and I reached a mutually beneficial arrangement."

Jeremiah considered what that might mean. What that sort of arrangement might involve. Leo? What would he have done for his brother? What would he have done for Cass? Anything. He thought of all the special doctors she required. The medicine. How did he pay for it all?

"People do what they have to do, Jeremiah. Don't judge them too harshly."

He had to clear his throat before he said, "Turn off your headlights. We're almost there."

39

Bill had approached the Murphy ranch from the east. Rico explained that it would likely be possible to get close without using roads. Looking at a map, there were no signs of creeks or streams in their way. As long as the scale was accurate they could approach and abandon the truck out of sight behind a hill and finish on foot.

It was slow going. Twice they hit impassable canyons and had to turn around. Then, in the distance, they saw it. A good-sized ranch house with a trailer close by on the property. They left the vehicle tucked behind a stand of bitter cherry trees. Bill carried the rifle in his hands, a pistol was tucked in his pants.

No activity was visible.

They came from the rear of the house. Toward the setting sun. As the sky dimmed, the windows of the house brightened. Shadows moved inside. But no sign of Leo Murphy's vehicle in the driveway. A black Jeep and a Honda Civic. An old barn, maybe an abandoned stable. It looked to Bill like he'd always pictured the house of sticks in the story of the three little pigs.

The image triggered flashes of Bill's childhood. Foster homes and foster parents. Mean and crazy times. Get tough or die times. He'd been plagued by nightmares, terrified of the dark. Afraid of what lurked under his bed or in the closet. But worse than the bogeymen of his imagination were the adults whose care he was in. The real monsters.

Those times had almost broken him. But he'd learned a valuable lesson.

The way to overcome one's fear of the bogeyman was to become the bogeyman. As he grew he stopped being afraid by making others fear him. He was the big bad wolf.

He told Rico to hide in the back of the pickup. Bill would be in the barn. When the sheriff returned they'd have him in a crossfire.

Bill was going to give this town something to be afraid of. A new monster. He wanted to populate the nightmares of every citizen here.

Rico crept to the truck, stayed low. Once he reached it he got in and laid down. He found a blue tarp there which he pulled over himself. Peeked at the house and waited.

Bill made his way to the barn which turned more sinister and inviting the closer he moved, the darker it got. The sun was a red bloodstain in a gray sky sinking below the mountains in the distance.

Leo hauled ass over the scarified roads to the

ranch. There'd been no answer when he called the home phone.

"Doesn't mean anything," Ryan said.

"It means something."

"It means nobody's answering the phone."

The light was fading fast. Dark descended from the west like an enormous pair of bat wings. He pushed down on the gas. Flashes of Three Js. The body pin-cushioned with wounds. His face a mask of agony. This was the handiwork of the man Ryan had invited into their lives. The creature that was probably already at Leo's house. His fingernails dug into his palms as he squeezed the life out of the steering wheel.

Next to him, Ryan checked his weapon. Rested it on his lap.

Almost all the light had seeped from the cloudy sky. They pulled into Leo's driveway. Everything glowed slightly crimson in the twilight. Jeremiah's old pickup was missing. Instead, Doris' sedan was parked near the house.

"You know that car?" Ryan asked.

"Doris. The waitress."

"Where's the pickup?"

"That's the question of the hour."

"Getting dark."

"Don't see any headlights."

Leo parked behind Doris' car. He hopped out and stepped forward to inspect it.

Ryan got out, gun drawn. The quickening in his

chest that always happened in combat. He sensed the closeness of death like an old friend. Everything slowed down.

Leo stepped in front of the car, lit clearly by the still shining headlights.

What a nice target he'd make, Ryan thought. Then he rushed forward and pulled his brother back just as the sound of a gunshot echoed.

Ryan felt the familiar burn and throb of a bullet wound in his left arm. He sucked in a breath.

They were on the ground, rolling back to the cover of the Explorer.

Another shot sent dirt flying inches away.

"He get you?"

"We gotta get inside."

"Christ, you're bleeding."

"Gotta turn off those headlights."

Leo opened the car door, grabbed the keys. Lights out.

"He must be in the barn. We need to get in around back or he'll have a clear shot at us."

"Count of three?"

"One. Two."

"Three."

They ran. More shots. A window shattered. A tire blew. They ran faster. Around back, Leo pulled the kitchen door open. Ryan slammed it behind him.

40

Cass let up a bit on the gas as they hit a sharp turn with a few big bumps. Doris gripped her rifle with her left hand and the handle on the door with her right and prayed that this little girl knew what the hell she was doing.

"Who taught you to drive?"

"My Papa."

Doris smiled and patted the .22 pistol on the seat between them. "He teach you how to use this too?"

Cass nodded. The road was smoother now. Doris breathed a sigh of relief.

"Where are we going?"

"The old mine entrance."

"What kind of mine?"

Cass didn't answer, or appear to hear the question. She did that every now and then.

"Cass, what kind of mine?"

"What?" As if she had forgotten Doris was there.

"What did they mine out of the ground?"

"I don't know. Nobody's used it in a long time."

The sky surrounding them, full of clouds lit from

behind, gradually vanished, turned black. It occurred to Doris that if a person were to get lost out here there'd be no possibility of finding your way until dawn. The thought made her shiver.

Cass kept her eyes straight ahead. "We're almost there."

Then what? Doris didn't dare ask out loud.

"Is your seatbelt on?"

"What?"

"Your seatbelt. Fasten it."

Doris pulled it across her and clicked it. "Guess I forgot in all the excitement."

Cass stomped on the brakes with both of her little feet. The old truck skidded to a stop, kicking up dirt and rocks. The rear window cracked between them as something from the bed of the truck crashed into it. A person.

Doris screamed.

Cass found the pistol on the floor by her feet and opened her door. "Run!" She pointed toward the mine entrance.

41

In the pitch-black house, Leo found the first aid kit blind. Brought it into the kitchen with Ryan.

"Motherfucker," Ryan repeated, like a mantra, changing which syllable he accented. "MOTHer-fucker. MotherFUCKer."

Leo couldn't see his brother's face but could picture the pained grimace as he cleaned out the wound. The peroxide fumes mingled with the rusty stink of blood.

"How bad is it?"

"Must have damaged a nerve. Can't move my arm. Help me put it in a sling."

Leo got a belt out of his bedroom. Ryan grunted when he pulled the left arm up and wrapped the belt around his neck. Ryan stood up, breathing hard.

When his breathing slowed, Leo whispered, "What's the play?"

"How about you wait here while I go after him."

"Nope."

"Didn't think so. That shot came from the barn.

So where is he now? He knows where we are. Smart play is for him not to be where we think he is."

Leo tried to concentrate but couldn't stop wondering where everybody else was. The truck was gone. Had they gotten away? He wiped his sweaty palms against his jeans, grateful for the darkness that kept it a secret.

"You scared?"

Leo didn't see much point in lying. They weren't children pretending to be tough. "There's a killer out there shooting at us. Don't know where Cass is. Or Dad. Or Doris. Yeah, I'm fucking scared."

"Me too. Like I was way back when. The night we dared each other to go out in the dark, barefoot. The night you got bit."

"The night you saved me."

"I was so scared."

"We were just kids."

"I was so scared I never moved."

"What are you talking about?"

Ryan let out a long, shaky breath, like he'd been holding it for thirty years. "I figured you'd get scared in a minute or two, come running back or call my name."

Too dark to see his face, Leo pictured his brother back then, just a boy. A scared boy. Before his eyes got hard.

"Why are you telling me this?"

"I wanted you to know. You were always the brave one, little brother."

A moment of silence. Leo's head spun with memories of that night, revising where Ryan was. But this new information didn't change what his brother had done in the end.

"It's okay. You still came through when it counted."

Ryan cleared his throat. "I had a time machine, there's a lot of things I'd go back and change. That's the first thing."

"But not the last?"

"Not the last."

Leo supposed this was Ryan's way of apologizing.

"So what are we gonna do now?"

"We go out the back door. One of us goes left. One goes right."

"Make our way to the barn."

"Yup. Use the dark against that city slicker. Figure we'll be quieter than him. One of us calls out or shoots, the other one comes guns blazing."

"Okay."

They crept to the kitchen. Slid the back door open. Slow and quiet. Ryan stepped out fast. Leo slid the door shut behind him. They stepped off the back porch. A sensation as familiar as a childhood nightmare.

Ryan went left.

Leo went right.

He knew Ryan felt it too. They'd seen this dark before.

42

The girls ran.

They headed toward the mine entrance, just an ominous blackness in the dark dark night. No idea what they would do when they got there. If they got there. The only thought, to get away from the man in the back of the truck. They found each other's hands.

Behind them, footsteps as the man staggered after them.

"Stop!" he yelled. "You will only make it worse girls."

Doris squeezed Cass' hand tighter.

The ground was uneven, sand and loose rocks. Cass stumbled. Doris tried to haul her up. *Don't stop, don't stop*. His footsteps got quicker, closer.

He pounced.

Doris let go of Cass' hand when the man tackled her. She landed hard, the wind knocked out of her, she couldn't scream, just moaned. Tried to tell Cass to run but it was only gibberish. His fists found her face. The ground was hard and sharp against the back of her head. *Please stop please stop please make it stop*. She tried to claw him, an animal noise hissed out of her mouth. Another blow to her temple. Everything a surprise, arriving out of the dark. He pinned her arms with his knees.

"Let her go."

The sound of a hammer being pulled back.

The punching stopped. In the wake of the truck headlights she could see his face now. Saw his eyes narrow as he turned toward Cass.

Impossible to see Cass' expression with the lights behind her.

"Didn't your daddy teach you not to play with guns?"

He got off Doris, who curled up and coughed. Her face already felt puffy from swelling. She tasted blood.

"Why don't you give me that? We don't want you."

We? Doris thought.

"Just hand it over and I'll take you home. Put you to sleep." His tone so soothing. "In the morning this'll feel like a bad dream. Maybe that's all this is."

Doris started to crawl away, tried to be quiet. Then her hand landed on the barrel of her rifle. Her father's words came to her. Aim for center mass. Squeeze, don't pull. Be ready to shoot again. She remembered herself as a little girl in a small town outside of Odessa. The pleasant smell of coffee on his breath as he leaned close.

The man made a lunge for Cass.

Doris fired.

Both of them kept their weapons pointed at the man's lifeless body. Grateful now for the dark.

But it didn't last.

Another set of headlights suddenly appeared, revealing the girls and the body on the ground between them. They looked at each other, faces red, eyes swollen, hair wild.

"What should we do?" Cass said.

Doris couldn't stop looking at the dead man. His eyes were still open, staring at her. Angry. A chill embraced her, made her teeth chatter. She kept expecting him to move, to jump at her like the killer always did in horror movies. One last scream.

The car continued to get closer. Police lights on top flashed red and blue.

"Doris?"

Finally she looked at Cass.

"Should we run?"

"I don't think I can." Her face ached, skin tight with swelling.

"Okay."

They waited until the car came to a stop next to the truck. From behind the lights came Jeremiah's voice.

"Girls, are you okay?"

"I don't know about okay," Doris said.

43

1980

"We walk straight out. You get scared, you get hurt, you call my name. Got it?" Ryan waited for an answer from the darkness. "You got it?"

"I got it." Leo's eight-year-old voice was shaky.

Ryan never took a step.

He waited right by the house and waited for his brother to get scared and call his name. He listened for Leo's soft bare footsteps. Hard to discern with the wind in his ears. He shuddered at the thought of walking out in the dark, barefoot.

The rattle was unmistakable. It turned his mouth to cotton.

He tried to call his brother's name but couldn't make a noise.

Leo howled in pain. So loud, it seemed to come from above, from everywhere.

Ryan turned the kitchen light on. Grabbed his father's shotgun. Saw two rounds in the chamber. Snapped it shut. He rushed outside. Leo was on the ground, not too far away. More screams. Ryan ran to him. Grabbed his shoulder.

"Did he get you?"

"It hurts, Ryan."

He never told anyone the whole truth. He burned with a coward's shame over it. Whenever his father scolded him about that night, Ryan knew in his heart that it was much worse than his father thought. He deserved all Jeremiah's scorn and a hell of a lot more.

Of all the nightmares that plagued him, the ones featuring Leo and the snake were the worst. His shame had driven him all his life. On the baseball diamond, in the military.

In the hospital, waiting to hear about his brother, his father angry and drunk and useless, Ryan swore he would never let his fear own him again.

Years later, in the army, his nickname would be mother duck. He always volunteered for the hard assignments. Never left a man behind. He was always counting the heads of his squad to make sure they were all accounted for. When one of his men was wounded, or worse, especially the younger ones, he saw Leo's boyish face, heard his screams.

44

2012

It was just too good an opportunity to pass up, Glenn thought.

When word of the contract had first reached him, he hadn't been able to think of a simple way to get involved. He figured Ryan would be up to his neck in it and had no desire to lock horns with the younger outlaw. Even for a hundred grand.

Then the call from Mrs. O'Leary. That sweet, dumb old lady.

So he headed to the Murphy ranch to see what there was to see. It fell right in his lap. Here was the waitress, the only remaining witness to the diner murder and he was pretty sure Mrs. O'Leary was harboring the shooter. Here they were, out in the middle of nowhere. Seeing the dead body, it occurred to him that he'd be able to pin the killings on the poor son of a bitch lying in the sand here.

There was really only one issue.

The young girl. Leo's daughter.

That went against even Glenn's admittedly crooked set of values.

But everything else was so perfect. He could even get rid of Jeremiah Murphy like he'd tried to all those years ago.

"I don't know about okay," the waitress said.

No, Glenn thought, very far from okay. But it'll all be over soon, sweetie.

Jeremiah rushed as fast as his old legs would carry him to his granddaughter.

"Who's that?" She pointed at Glenn, who gave her his best smile.

"That's Glenn. Sheriff of Quicksilver."

Hard to make out her features in the dimness. She seemed to give him a skeptical squint. Glenn had heard she was a little touched.

Glenn drew his pistol and walked over to the body. A throwdown piece he kept handy for just such an occasion. He knelt and checked for a pulse. None. Lots of blood. The air was thick with the smell of it.

"Looks like you got him," he said to the waitress.

She was in pretty rough shape. Face all banged up. Left eye nearly swollen shut. The thing to do was get Jeremiah first. There was a rifle next to the girl but too far for her to get at quick enough.

Jeremiah was asking his granddaughter questions but she wasn't answering.

She didn't take her eyes off Glenn.

It made him nervous.

She seemed to know what he was going to do before he did it. Maybe he was just spooking himself. His conscience nagging at him. Maybe.

Now or never, he thought.

Now.

He lifted his arm to fire.

"Papa, look out!" She pulled him to the ground.

"Dammit," Glenn hissed when the shot missed.

"Run, Cass!" Jeremiah shouted and rolled into the dark.

Glenn tried to fire where he thought Jeremiah was. Then he aimed at Doris, who scrambled for her rifle.

Cass didn't run. She spread her legs, centered Glenn in her gun sight, exhaled, and squeezed the trigger.

The bullet hit him right in the heart, knocked him to the ground. His last thought as he stared up at the pitch sky was how cold the desert could get at night. He died shivering.

45

Ryan heard gunshots in the distance, like miniature thunder claps. Pistol shots, he thought. It reminded him of his days in the Middle East, where the distant racket of Kalashnikovs was as common as mosquitoes buzzing back home.

He moved forward. Slowly. Through the void. His pistol pointed forward, leading the way. His eyes strained but they might as well have been closed. He relied on his ears to warn him of danger. His memory drew in the details, the house, the barn, conjured his boyhood fears, the dark, snakes, scorpions. An image of the ground littered with creatures nearly made him freeze.

He forced his feet to move. Carefully. Softly. One step at a time.

Leo heard the gunshots too. What the hell could that be? Came from the north. In the direction of the old family mine. Impossible not to feel a bit like the boy who went out into a night this black thirty years ago. There were still monsters in the dark, this time a man named Bill. He was grateful tonight for his boots. What a stupid kid he'd been. All balls, no brains. Here he was again. Walking out into the dark with his brother, courting danger. He tried to focus on the task at hand. Don't think about snakes, or the girls or Jeremiah. Someone had shot Ryan. Probably Bill. Listen, he told himself. Watch. Be ready.

Quietly, he moved toward the barn, just the slightest bit blacker than the sky behind it.

Thunder boomed, the breeze picked up, the scent of rain in the thick air.

Bill had never seen anything like this dark. He felt submerged in night. The sounds were all foreign to him, nothing familiar. Dizzy, he decided to crawl on all fours toward where he thought the house was. He tried not to think about the all-too-likely possibility that he could be headed in the opposite direction.

The memory of being burned in a car in Miami occurred to him. The helpless feeling, thinking his number was up. Where was Rico? He should've taken care of them by now. A couple of girls and two old cops. He could handle that. Bill's knees were getting sore. It was awkward, holding his pistol as he crawled.

Bill didn't recognize what the sound was at first.

He'd only ever heard it in movies or TV shows. Never in real life. The air was filled with the electric noise of a rattlesnake's warning. Bill jerked back on his feet, stumbling on jagged rocks and loose stones and sand.

The snake's threat made Leo's leg throb and tingle like one of Pavlov's dogs salivating at the sound of a bell. He heard footsteps stumble, a man cried out in surprise and fear. Bill. Might even be the same spot as years ago, he thought. Leo willed himself to turn toward the sound of the scared rattler. Like a fireman moves to a burning building.

Ryan heard it. Their old friend the rattlesnake. He moved slow and deliberate, scanning back and forth with his eyes and his pistol for something to see, something to shoot at.

Bill shook with fright, sensed a warm wetness in his crotch as he pissed himself. Waved his sidearm wildly at the phantom snakes his mind painted in the darkness. The rattling grew in intensity, got louder, angrier. His ears invented the sounds of hissing, slithering. Every second he expected to feel a bite. He fired, blindly, at the snake.

Then, headlights.

***

Christ, Ryan thought. The same damn pickup I drove Leo to the hospital in thirty years ago. The deja vu juju of this night just got weirder and weirder. The beams sliced through the thick blackness, bounced up and down as the truck moved closer. Ryan zeroed in on the spaces the headlights exposed, waited for Bill to appear, raised his pistol. Steadied his breathing.

As soon as light shone on the snake, its eyes glowed, fangs sparkled, Bill shot it in the head. Then he ducked as a shot missed him. The lights moved past him and flashed on Leo.

The truck came to a stop.

Leo stood, blinded, in the spotlights.

Ryan scanned the area where he'd seen Bill shoot the snake, eyes straining for movement.

"Daddy!" Cass started running for Leo.

"Cass, stop!" Jeremiah shouted.

There. Bill's arm came up. He aimed.

Ryan shot first.

And last.

He stepped closer. Cautious. Just enough light to see that Bill had fallen next to the snake. Ryan shot each of them one more time.

Jeremiah and Doris stepped into the circle of light centered on Leo and Cass embracing. Ryan felt a tug to join them but ignored it. Stayed where he was. This was all his fault. He'd set all of this in motion. He still had some loose ends to tie up if he wanted to keep the people in that circle of light safe.

He walked to his Jeep. Started it up. Drove north, to the mine entrance. The rain started, fast and hard. It wasn't too far. He turned off the car lights and stepped out into the night suddenly exhausted. It was always the same after a battle. He was physically and mentally spent. His wound barked at him. He'd need to find a doctor over the border. He knew a man. He'd live. Lord knew Ryan had survived worse.

Thunder growled. The lightning revealed a Quicksilver police cruiser. Another flash and a closer look showed the bodies of Rico and Glenn. Ryan stood stunned in the rain for a moment. "I'll be damned."

Once Leo stepped inside the mine, darkness and silence embraced him. Like old friends.

Relief flooded Leo's heart. Cass was safe. He saw Jeremiah and Doris walking closer. He squeezed Cass harder. She shook in his arms.

"It's okay now. It's okay."

He let her cry.

When Jeremiah was close enough, he said,

"Where's Ryan?"

An engine turned on. Ryan's Jeep drove away.

Just as well. Still, he'd saved Leo's ass again. Even if this was all his fault, that counted for something. Didn't mean he wouldn't take a few swings at him the next time he came to town.

Doris kept away, avoided turning her face toward Leo.

"Is she okay?"

"She got a little roughed up," Jeremiah said.

"How?"

"We had some trouble with a bad man too. Didn't we, Cass?"

Leo felt her sob harder. "Two bad men."

"What happened?"

"Son, we've got some cleaning up to do."

Then the storm descended. The night wept and shuddered, rain like bullets clattered on the roofs of the house and the cars, whipped against their faces. It was as though all the emotions swirling inside Leo had been released into the air. Thunder bawled, the sky was torn by seams of jagged lightning. Terrible and beautiful and dangerous, like most things in this godforsaken land. Leo prayed that this brief rain would stop a fire from starting, prayed that Cass wouldn't be too scarred by this incident, even prayed that Ryan was okay.

Couldn't remember the last time one of his prayers had been answered.

46

Ryan landed in Miami on a hot, humid Thursday. He rented a bright red Chevy Impala. Everything was bright in Miami. Even the sun seemed brighter here, the sky bluer. He drove to Coral Gables, to Don Palermo's house, and waited. Around three o'clock a black Mercedes sedan with tinted windows glided out of the gates of the driveway.

He followed.

The Mercedes zoomed through the palm-tree-lined streets into Little Havana. Parked at the curb in front of a tiny cigar shop on Calle Ocho.

Ryan drove past and parked a few dozen yards down the street. He adjusted his rearview mirror to better observe the scene.

Don Palermo got out of the car and headed inside alone.

His instincts told him this was his best bet. Catch him alone in a public place. He got out of the car, strolled to the cigar shop as nonchalant as he could manage.

The pleasant smells of tobacco and leather inside.

Latin jazz played low in the background. Palermo sat in a leather chair beside a small circular table with an ashtray on it. He puffed on a thick, short stogie. Ryan walked in front of him and removed his sunglasses. Waited for recognition in Palermo's eyes. After a few seconds, it clicked. The older man shook his head.

"I never expected to see you again, pal. At least not alive."

Ryan pointed to the chair on the other side of the table.

Palermo chuckled, but said, "Be my guest. Have a seat. How about a smoke? This is the best shop in town."

"Thanks, but no thanks."

"So you're not here to smoke. Why are you here?"

"To apologize."

"Apologize? Ain't that polite of you. Really. I'm getting choked up. Yeah, Mr. Palermo, I know not one fucking thing about my plan worked. And I know your best man is now taking a dirt nap, but, shucks, I'm awful sorry."

Ryan let him talk. Let him get it off his chest.

Palermo chewed on his cigar. Narrowed his eyes at Ryan. "You think killers like Bill grow on fucking palm trees, asshole?"

"No, sir." He was grateful they didn't.

"Fucking A right, no, sir." Palermo's face had turned red.

Ryan noticed the nervous glances of the staff.

"How do I make it up to you?"

"You're here to make it up to me?"

"Yup."

More chuckles. "First, why the hell would I trust you to do a goddamn thing? Second, Teddy McCarthy's still running around after killing Sal. Still one live witness to that killing. So he gets picked up, he can connect the dots to me. That's no good. No good at all. If you want to save somebody, you have to kill somebody."

"So Teddy or the witness has to go?"

"You've got a real grasp of the obvious."

"Thanks."

"Now Teddy at least completed the task he was hired for. So he's due some money."

"Give him the money before I take care of him?"

"Assuming you choose him. Find out what he wants done with it."

"You're serious?"

"I'm always serious. Come by the house tomorrow. We'll get you the cash."

"How do you know I won't keep Teddy's money?"

Palermo puffed on his cigar. "You got a few too many scruples. That's why you're here. Setting things right, making sure I don't go after your family." Palermo relit his stogie. "It'll be your downfall."

"Maybe."

"Being good at it isn't enough sometimes. Guys like Bill, no conscience, no qualms. They scare the shit out of people. Hell, he scared the shit out of me. Guys like you and Teddy, you're nice to have around. Loyal. But there's lines you won't cross. Sometimes you need to cross those lines."

"So take care of Teddy. Take care of the money. That's it?"

"No, that's not fucking it. You took out my number one killer. You owe me one job. Whoever I say. Whenever I say."

Ryan stood. "I'll be in touch."

"I'll be here."

47

The town of Las Lápidas was barely a town. It didn't show up on most maps. A few dozen adobe homes, a general store, and a ragged tavern that looked held together by glue and prayer.

The old gringo sat in his usual seat at a table on the front stoop of the tavern. He sipped on a tequila and ate some rice and beans with a fresh tortilla— his usual breakfast. He didn't speak much Spanish. His interactions with the citizens of Las Lápidas consisted mostly of nods and gestures. Always a por favor and a gracias.

This morning he was writing on the back of a postcard. He ended it the way he always ended them. *This will probably be the last card I write.* After he signed his name he looked up and saw the man in the doorway. Another gringo. He offered him a weak smile and a sigh.

"You look like your brother."

"You're a hard man to find."

The old man chuckled.

"Something funny?"

"Just having a case of deja vu."

"But from the other side of things."

Teddy nodded. "What was the original plan? Once I got across the border?"

"It was pretty simple. It didn't turn out well for you."

Teddy took a deep breath. "Will he leave them alone? Is that the deal? Did he tell you, if you want to save somebody, you have to kill somebody?"

"That's the way it seems to work, isn't it?"

"Doing the wrong thing for the right reason is still the wrong thing. It weighs on a man. Chips away at his soul. Until there ain't nothing left."

"You finished?"

He held up the postcard. "Will you see that gets delivered?"

"I will. You've got something else that might need delivering. A payment for services rendered. Does it go to the same address?" His pistol was aimed at the old man now.

Teddy nodded. "Palermo always paid his debts." He looked at Ryan, at the gun, then took in his surroundings, as if he wanted to remember every detail. "I've often wondered how this would go down."

"Just like this."

"I guess I'll see you in hell, Ryan Murphy."

The two gunshots echoed through the quiet town.

"I'm sure you will."

The couple who ran the tavern remained in the kitchen while Ryan put some money on the table and picked Teddy's postcard up off the floor. As he walked to his car parked down the road, he could sense the villagers peeking at him from the corners of windows. Inside his Jeep he told himself he'd had to do it. To protect his family. This didn't make him feel better about it. He knew the truth. His own greed had caused all of this. His father had been right. He made a living out of people dying.

How many men were waiting in Hell for him now? He'd lost count.

48

Leo and Cass took the Kumeyaay Highway west. She wanted to know where they were going.

"I like to keep my promises," was all Leo would say.

She was having a tough time since that night with all the killing. Quiet in the day. Loud at night, when she woke from her bad dreams. She hadn't slept through a night in the weeks that had passed.

"I'm here," he called when he woke to her screams. He would limp to her room, his leg always tricky when he first woke. "I'm here. It's okay. Just a nightmare."

More memories than nightmares. A reliving of what happened. What she did. In her dreams she pulled the trigger over and over. The stranger died again and again.

Leo knew she needed counseling. A professional ear to listen to her.

But they hadn't exactly gone by the book that night. Wicked Bill and his flunky and Glenn were buried under six feet of sand and rock at the edge of Murphy land. Leo had driven Glenn's cruiser north to the edge of Quicksilver in the middle of the night while Jeremiah and Cass followed in Leo's Explorer. Leo poured gas all over it and lit it on fire.

All facts Leo wasn't anxious for Cass to share with a therapist.

She was quiet, stared out at the Kumeyaay Reservation as it passed on the right. Hills of creosote bushes and cacti. "I think this is the farthest I've ever been from home."

"I suppose you're right."

"You think this is the way Mom went?"

"Probably."

"I try to picture her sometimes. What she's doing. Where she is." She shrugged. "It's hard to picture though. You know? Because I haven't really been anywhere. So I picture her in scenes from movies."

"I think about her too. I wonder the same things."

"I picture her coming back home. I have a dream where I get off the bus and walk inside and there she is."

"What does she say?"

She turned and looked at him. "It's always different. 'Hey stranger.' Or, 'Where you been, Cass?'" Tears in her eyes.

He reached his hand out, put it on the back of her neck.

"Right here, Mom. I've been right here the whole time." Her body shook with weeping.

"I have that dream all the time."

"Really?"

"The worst ones are when I wake up and think she's still living with us. For a few minutes, I wonder where she is. Then I remember, she's gone."

"Do you think she misses us?"

"I hope so. I hope she misses us so bad it hurts."

They crossed into San Diego County. In Viejas they stopped at a casino to use the bathroom and get a drink.

"Not long now," he said.

"Where are we going?"

"West."

She rolled her eyes. "Thanks. Very helpful."

"You're welcome."

After they passed El Cajon, traffic thickened. Leo kept going until he reached the exit for the 5 north.

"Is that the ocean?" She pointed across her father at Mission Bay.

"Not quite."

They drove north. At Mount Soledad they merged onto La Jolla Parkway. The road curved west through gorgeous neighborhoods of white stucco homes packed tight together, outfitted with pools and tennis courts. Palm trees and torrey pines lined the streets.

Up ahead, just above the tops of the trees, the endless blue of the ocean.

"There it is."

Cass was speechless.

Leo turned right onto La Jolla Shores Drive then

wound his way left and right until he got to a parking lot next to the beach.

Cass couldn't take her eyes from the ocean. She lowered her window. She could see the waves crashing now, hear them. The smell of salt was overwhelming.

Leo parked next to Ryan's black jeep. Not sure how this was going to go. Leo's gaze was drawn to the water too. You saw it on the TV and in movies but the ocean wasn't just something to see. He took a deep breath of sea air into his lungs, savored the feeling.

They got out of the car. Leo removed his shoes and socks, Cass kicked off her sandals. The sand was hot on their bare feet. The beach was nearly deserted at noon on a Monday.

The ocean drew them close until they stopped, dazzled, by the sun, the ocean's blue, the sound of the waves crashing, the wind on their faces. As if they had walked into a postcard.

"Impressive, isn't it?"

Ryan was in board shorts and a t-shirt.

"What are you doing here, Uncle Ryan?"

Leo watched her for signs of distress. Would his brother trigger bad memories?

"I wanted to be here. The first time either of you saw the ocean."

Her eyes followed a sea gull as it dove into the water for a fish. "This was your idea?"

He scratched the stubble on his face. "If you're

going to do something, you might as well do it right. This is the prettiest spot I could think of that you two could drive to."

"Did you bring me a present, Uncle Ryan?"

"You know I did." He held a short board with a floral pattern on it. "They call it a boogie board."

Leo cleared his throat. "I have a bathing suit in the back of the car."

Ryan pointed to a bag on a towel. "That's what we talked about. Be obliged if you could deliver it."

Leo picked up the bag and walked back toward the parking lot.

Cass moved to the edge of the water, paused to look left and right, up and down the vast shoreline squinting at the sun's reflection, then stepped into a cascading wave.

Ryan took off his shirt, threw it on the sand, and followed her. A fresh scar from that night on his left arm, to go with the dozens of older wounds on his arms and torso. She touched the newest one, the flesh puckered and pink.

"Do they make you sad?"

"That one does. I'm so sorry, Cass. For what I put you and your father through."

Leo remained back on the beach, a hard expression on his face.

Cass looked from her father to her uncle to the ocean. "I have dreams about it."

"I do too."

She pointed to his other wounds. "Do they all

give you bad dreams?"

"They all have a story. And then there's the scars you can't see." He pointed to his head.

"I think I have some of those too."

Ryan nodded. "Those can take the longest to heal."

He could still remember the first time he'd killed a person. The Battle of Wadi-Al Batin. Operation Knight Strike. A cold desert night in February. One of the Abrams M1 tanks got disabled after an ambush. Ryan and another four men in a Bradley rushed to their aid. The sound of bullets ricocheting. Off the Abrams. Off the Bradley.

An Iraqi tank had moved up close.

The M1 couldn't move but could still fire. Their M681 scored a direct hit on the enemy tank. Then took a mortar round itself.

Soldiers scrambled out of both tanks. Shadowy silhouettes against the sky. The Americans moved low toward the Bradley. Ryan and his crew covered them, shooting toward the enemy tank. One by one they hopped into the Bradley.

"Is that everyone?" the sergeant asked.

"Arnold's still back there. He was up near the blast. Told us he'd catch up."

Ryan didn't hesitate. Hopped out of the Bradley and sprinted toward the crippled, smoldering Abrams.

"Don't forget to drop a grenade, Murphy. Scuttle the tank," the sergeant called after him.

Strange to be out in the open. Sand under his

feet. Stars bright above him. Like home. Weird to be aware of his own breathing in the middle of a battle. The weapon blasts seemed distant, unrelated.

He needed to get Arnold. Blow the tank. Get back to the Bradley. That was it. That was the mission now.

Flames from the Abrams made it visible.

He hopped up onto the metal and inside.

Moans.

Deep and awful. He moved to the front of the tank and found Arnold. What was left of him. An orgy of gore for the senses. The smell of charred flesh. Arnold's legs were mostly ash. Everything below the waist was gone, melted, still bubbling. The heat far worse than the desert sun, close and smoky. And the sounds of Arnold moaning and his skin sizzling.

Ryan vomited.

Arnold's voice was a strangled whisper. "Make it stop."

Ryan gently suffocated him with a towel.

His first killing was a mercy killing.

Gagging, he pulled Arnold out of the tank. Arnold's half a body was too light.

He encountered two enemies on his way back to the Bradley, but Ryan was too quick. Hit both men in the chest. Barely saw them as he rushed in the dark to the hulking safety of his vehicle.

Couldn't sleep for days after. Haunted by what he'd witnessed in that tank. By what he'd had to do.

Haunted like Cass would be now. He watched her step deeper into the Pacific. How could this skinny girl have killed a man? Not a little girl any-more.

She squinted in the sun when she turned to look at him. "Do they ever go away?"

Ryan held out his arms, displayed his scar tissue. "No. But they fade over time, if you let them."

"How?"

"You try to replace them with good memories."

"Try to forget them."

"No. You won't forget. Neither will I or your dad. You know what I can't forget?"

"What?"

"How brave you were. How you saved Papa's life. Remember that, Cass."

She shivered in the breeze. "Remember it, but don't talk about it."

"You can always talk about it with me. Or your dad. Or Papa."

"Like a club."

"I suppose."

"Of people who've killed people."

"You did what you had to do, Cass. You were in the wrong place at the wrong time. But you did the right thing."

"It scares me."

"What scares you?"

Her face turned flat, secretive. She shook her head. He paused, not sure he wanted to unlock this door. But wasn't it his fault? All of this. "I won't tell anyone, kid. This is just you and me."

She watched a wave retreat to the ocean, leaving her feet covered in sand up to her ankles. Then she looked up at him, a gaze too old for her years, a stare he'd seen in soldiers after battle, in criminals after a successful heist.

"I liked it."

A storm of seagulls whirled in the air behind her, their wails echoed in the darkest recesses of his mind. She turned and dove into a wave.

Ryan moved to the water's edge, next to Leo.

"How is she?"

"Not great."

Cass dove again. They watched and waited for her to surface. She was one of them now.

She had learned the hard way that as long as they lived, the hits would keep on coming.

Their eyes were open to the darkness of the world. They knew how close death was. It was a heavy burden to live with.

Then Cass' head emerged from the ocean and they all savored this rare moment of light.

ACKNOWLEDGMENTS

I can't thank Chris Rhatigan enough for giving this novel a home when I wondered if it would ever find one.

MIKE MINER lives is the author of six books, including *True Dark*, *Hurt Hawks*, and *Prodigal Sons*. His short fiction has been published in a variety of magazines and anthologies as well as two collections, *The Hurt Business* and *Everything She Knows*. His stories have twice been listed as "Other Distinguished Mystery Stories" in the *Best American Mystery Stories* series. He lives in New England.

On the following pages are a few
more great titles from the
Down & Out Books publishing family.

For a complete list of books and to
sign up for our newsletter,
go to DownAndOutBooks.com.

Skunk Train
Joe Clifford

Down & Out Books
December 2019
978-1-64396-055-5

Starting in the Humboldt wilds and ending on the Skid Row of Los Angeles, *Skunk Train* follows two teenagers, who stumble upon stolen drug money, with drug dealers, dirty cops, and the Mexican mob on their heels.

On a mission to find his father, Kyle heads to San Francisco, where he meets Lizzie Decker, a wealthy high school senior, whose father has just been arrested for embezzlement. Together, Kyle and Lizzie join forces, but are soon pursued by Jimmy, the two dirty cops, and the Mexican cartel, as a third detective closes in, attempting to tie loose threads and solve the Skunk Train murders.

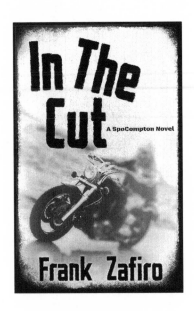

In the Cut
A SpoCompton Crime Novel
Frank Zafiro

Down & Out Books
January 2020
978-1-64396-075-3

Boone's quest to join the Iron Brotherhood outlaw motorcycle gang comes to a head after a dangerous encounter he faces on the club's behalf. His reward comes with even greater danger, in the form of drugs, violence, and dark relationships.

When the person who is the closest thing he has to family dies, Boone's world explodes, and he learns what it really means to live life…in the cut.

Countdown
Matt Phillips

All Due Respect, an imprint of
Down & Out Books
978-1-948235-84-6

LaDon and Jessie—two hustlers who make selling primo weed a regular gig—hire a private security detail to move and hold their money. Ex-soldiers Glanson and Echo target the cash—they start a ripoff business. It's the wild, wild west. Except this time, everybody's high.

With their guns and guts, Glanson and Echo don't expect much trouble from a mean son-of-a-gun like LaDon Charles. But that's exactly what they get. In this industry, no matter how much money there is for the taking—and no matter who gets it—there's always somebody counting backwards...to zero.

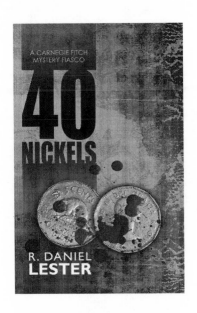

40 Nickels
A Carnegie Fitch Mystery Fiasco
R. Daniel Lester

Shotgun Honey, an imprint of
Down & Out Books
978-1-948235-16-7

Carnegie Fitch can be called a lot of things. Ambitious is not one of them.

Months after escaping death in the circus ring at the hands of the Dead Clowns and the feet of a stampeding elephant, he is no longer a half-assed private eye with an office and no license, but instead a half-assed tow truck driver without either. Still, he daydreams about landing that BIG CASE.

Well, careful what you wish for, Fitch.